THE ENLIGHTENING
THE MACKENZIE DUNCAN SERIES

Star Bound Books

Other titles by Adrianne James

Young Adult Titles:
Life on Loan
Overexposed

Series:
The Mackenzie Duncan Series
The Tempering: Book 1
The Enlightening: Book 2

Coming Soon:
Coming Home Series
(NA Contemporary Romance)
The Billionaire and The Barfly: Book 1

The Enlightening
Mackenzie Duncan Series
By Adrianne James

Copyright 2013 by Adrianne James
Published by Star Bound Books

Cover Design by Gonet Design
http://www.facebook.com/gonetdesign
Editing by Rogena Mitchell-Jones Manuscript Service
http://www.RogenaMitchell.com

Acknowledgements

This book wouldn't be what it is today without my editor, Rogena Mitchell-Jones and my wonderful betas, Nicki DeStasi and Amber Vaugn. Rachael from Mark My Words Book Publicity has helped to get this book and me out there so you could find me. And as always, JC Emery, my writing buddy, my sounding board, my best friend.

To my parents: Thank you for always believing in me. Your words of encouragement and praise have kept me going whenever I felt like giving up. I love you both.

To my readers: I appreciate each and every one of you.

ONE

Liam Hardy had been complaining about the cold since they had left the pack house three days prior. The snow was cold, his socks were wet, and his nose was tingling from the wind chill. All of which was bullshit in Mackenzie's opinion. They were Werewolves and the heat that radiated from within their bodies made sure they never felt the sting of the cold.

"Let's head west. I'm fucking tired of the cold."

"West doesn't mean warm. South means warm," Geoff bit back. Tensions were running on high between the two men. It could have possibly had something to do with the fact that both wanted Mackenzie and she couldn't pick between the two. Or it could have something to do with the fact that they were all used to living in a huge house with all the amenities and left it behind with nothing more than a backpack each. They had been sleeping wherever they could manage and still didn't have an actual plan as to what they were going to be doing now that they were considered rogue.

"Of course it does! Everyone says California is hot. They have mild winters and hot summers. California is west." The boys had stopped walking long enough to glare at one another. Mackenzie was sick and tired of it. She wasn't their mother, or either of their girlfriends, so why did she have to step in and take care of them?

"Will the both of you just chill the fuck out? Let's go Southwest okay? It's a little thing called a compromise, boys. Figure it out, or I will leave the both of you and find my own way. Oh and Liam, you know I adore your face just the way it is, but if you complain one more god damn time about your nose being too cold, I will rip it off. We radiate heat. If you need to complain about something, at least be honest about it."

"And what would something honest be?" Liam looked at her with a mix of adoration and irritation. It was an interesting combo, that's for sure. He wore his feelings on his sleeve and was still a young wolf, much like her, whose emotions could shift in point two seconds if given a reason. Hell, even without a real reason.

"Let's see, we have been walking for three days and have yet to actually stay in a real building. The only food we have eaten was hunted by Wolfy Geoff, so it was mangled to bits by the time he brought it back to be cooked. And the two of you stink. Big time. Didn't either of you think to pack deodorant?"

Mackenzie was just as annoyed with their situation as the boys, but she didn't see any reason to openly complain at every turn. Liam did. His looks would only get him so far with her patience, and with his blonde hair, blue eyes, and sculpted abs, that was actually quite far. Geoff on the other hand was dark where Liam was light. He was just as gorgeous but also had hundreds of years of experience under his belt to help him with his maturity. If only that maturity flowed into his romantic life, they would have been together a long time ago.

"What are you talking about? We smell like roses!" Geoff said from behind her through a hearty laugh. Liam glared at him for a moment before laughing along with him.

"You might want to be careful who you call stinky, Mac. You are not too far behind us." Then Liam ran. It was a smart move because Mackenzie was right behind him.

"Sure, leave me to grab the bags!" Geoff called out after them. When Mackenzie glanced over her shoulder, she watched him lift both hers and Liam's bag onto his shoulders. His strength had always impressed her, and she could imagine the way his muscles were moving and flexing beneath his long sleeved shirt. Licking her lips, she remembered just a week before when those muscles were rippling beneath her fingers as she explored his chest.

Geoff smirked at her and blew a kiss in her direction. Mackenzie shook her head to rid her mind of his gorgeous body and talented tongue. She had been the one to stop things. She had been the one to say that until she knew who she wanted, Geoff or Liam, it wasn't right to be with either in that way. Both men agreed with her, much to her surprise. She had fully expected one to tell her to fuck off. She knew that if she had been one of two girls vying for the affection of a man she might be a little pissed that he couldn't choose.

"Geoff, what's the hold up?" Liam called from a few feet in front of her. Mackenzie turned back around and took off after him again. He wasn't expecting it, and since she was the faster runner, she tackled him without even trying.

"I do not stink. Let's get out of the damn woods and find a real place to stay for once?"

"I don't know, I think I like you right here," Liam whispered, keeping his hands firmly on her hips. She rolled her eyes and stood up just as Geoff caught up with them.

"Good idea. Real food should be on the agenda, as well."

"Agenda? Who talks like that?" Liam asked under his breath. He wasn't taking things as well as Geoff was. Perhaps Geoff just had more confidence, or maybe Liam just cared more. He had never pushed her away like Geoff had. Well, at least he hadn't once he was done trying to kill her. Turning a perfectly wonderful human into a blood thirsty monster sort of dampens the lovey-dovey feelings.

"I do. Let's just go." Geoff took the lead, which Mackenzie was more than happy with. She was sick and tired of looking at snow covered ground and bare trees. She wanted a real bed and a hot shower and possibly three or four plates full of pancakes and eggs.

~*~

The motel was run down and rather sketchy looking. If it weren't for the two men on either side of her, and for her super strength thanks to her new wolf genes, she might actually be afraid to step through the doorway. But they were and she was, so Mackenzie opened the door to what she guessed they considered a lobby to rent a room.

"Is this place really where we should be staying? I mean, I bet we can find a hotel if we go further into town." Geoff was looking around in disgust. It made her laugh a little at how uncomfortable he was. She wasn't sure if he was worried about the possible crime or if he just wanted his normal accommodations of king size beds, room service, and a maid. Geoff was kind of a slob on his own.

"This is what we can afford. Seriously, it's not that bad. We have all stayed in worse, and after three days in the woods, anything with a mattress is perfect for me." Geoff and Liam shared a look then with a shrug went back to inspecting the area. A creak from behind the desk alerted them to the fact that they were no longer alone.

An old man with no hair on his head, but a full white beard on his face, hobbled into the room. He nodded at Mackenzie then found his seat. The legs of the chair screeched against the linoleum floor, sending a shiver down her spine. It was almost like nails on a chalk board.

"How many?" The old man's voice was harsh. It sounded like someone who hadn't had a drink of anything in days. He coughed a few times and cleared his throat, but nothing helped him.

"Just the three of us. One room please, with two beds if you have it?"

"Got a room with one bed or you can get two rooms."

"One bed is fine. I'm sure we can manage." Mackenzie looked behind her at Geoff and Liam hoping they would agree, but they stared at her instead. Then they looked at each other and groaned. They knew they would either have to share the bed with her together, or sleep on the floor. She had a feeling she knew what they would choose and it was stupid.

"Room 103. Thirty dollars."

Mackenzie pulled the money from her bag and handed it over. She didn't know if either of the other two had any. She really didn't know anything about what they were doing, where they were going, or what they would do when they got there. How had they gone three days without really saying anything to each other? It was time to really sit down and talk, and as much as it needed to be done, it was not going to go over well.

~*~

The springs squeaked loudly as Mackenzie sat down on the floral print blanket that adorned the double bed in the center of the small motel room. Geoff and Liam stood awkwardly in separate corners of the tiny space looking anywhere but at her on the bed, or at each other.

"So," Mackenzie began. She looked up to Geoff first, his dark eyes penetrating the stain in the carpet just in front of his foot, then to Liam, who was studying the poster on the bathroom door of how to get out in case of an emergency.

"So," both Liam and Geoff spoke at the same time, glancing at one another then quickly away.

"This has got to be talked about. What? Are we going to keep traveling together in complete and total silence or awkward conversations? We are all mature adults. I'm sure we aren't the first to find ourselves in this situation, right?"

"Is that supposed to be a joke?" Geoff looked up, irritation in his eyes. "Three werewolves caught in a love triangle, because one can't decide between the one who gave up his home and family of two hundred years for her and the one who is tied to her by a sire bond? Which do you think is real, Mackenzie?"

"Hey! It has nothing to do with the fact that she is my sire. If you remember correctly, I hated her for that exact fact!" Liam's whole body was shaking with tension. Mackenzie knew she needed to cool the situation down before he lost control, not that Geoff couldn't handle it, if he did.

"I meant when three friends have feelings for each other and they don't know what to do. That has happened to so many damn people in this world that just about a quarter of all romance books and movies are about that exact thing! And no, most aren't supernatural beings, but being a wolf doesn't change the fact that we are together right now, all three of us. I meant, we need to talk about what we are going to do about our… the pack? Are they really just letting us go? Would Margret give you up that easy?" The last part was directed at Geoff. He knew the wolfy politics and he knew Margret. Probably better than anyone else.

"So we ignore the attraction, both physical and emotional, for now and focus on keeping our asses alive. As long as we keep our heads down and don't interfere with her plans, I am pretty sure we will be fine. It might be a good idea to go somewhere out of her areas, though."

"Where would that be? Sounds like she is working on taking over the whole United States." Liam sat on the floor with his legs tucked under him, his back against the wall and his head leaning back, eyes trained on the ceiling. With a quick look up, Mackenzie knew he was counting the tiles. He did that when he was trying to keep his cool.

"There are other descendants of the other Weres. Margret's mother, had siblings. They never became powerful like she was as they were the younger siblings. Much like human royalty, only the eldest female gets to attain the crown," Geoff explained.

"The eldest female? Aren't monarchies usually lead by the men?" Liam asked

"They are the ones who can guarantee a legitimate offspring. When Rosalinda, Margret's mother, was killed, her siblings decided it would be for the better to allow each family to run itself with a few guidelines. They sent messages out in hopes that they could all live how they wanted and be better able to hide and keep everyone safe. Rosalinda's wolves, her guard, I guess you could call them, had been sloppy. Arrogant. They were being spotted by humans left and right and were turning people without even a worry of who it was to be turned. If each family governed themselves, then perhaps they would learn from the mistakes of their deceased queen and would protect the secret."

"So, before her was another King and Queen and they died. Did they run things the same way that Rosalinda did?" Mackenzie was fascinated. None of her research on the mythology of Lycanthropes told this story. Even Liam had leaned forward, listening intently.

"Correct and no. Rosalinda was heartbroken after her parent's death and thought that the wolves of the world should have protected her parents instead of killing them. There were rogues that didn't want to live under a ruler. They wanted to feast whenever they wanted, and mate whenever they wanted with whomever they wanted, and there were strict rules about that back then. So when Rosalinda took over, she really took over. She executed any who would go against her or spoke ill of her parents. She began turning humans to create her army and even infiltrated the human royalty by marrying a duke and having an affair with the King.

"She wanted power and obedience. She was the exact opposite of her parents in that way. They wanted harmony and safe living amongst the humans, which was the reason for the rules. Rosalinda had a daughter. She planned on having at least one more child, but had hoped to have the King's offspring, but her wolves were becoming overly aggressive and sloppy in their procurement of new pups, and the humans began the hunt. She was killed by her own husband while Margret, only a small child, was in the back bedroom.

"As Margret aged, she noticed the changes in herself and was so grateful that her father did not. When she turned for the first time, she killed him. She had always known what she was and knew that she had to keep it a secret from everyone after watching her mother bleed to death on their stone kitchen floor. She ran in the middle of the night to where her mother spoke of family living, and they took her in, teaching her how to be a wolf. They taught her to be an example to other wolves that still respected the fallen queen, and by default, looked to her for guidance

"After a while, she became restless. Wanting to take action against those who had been so careless to be caught, and in the end, get her mother killed. No one would tell her. No one knows if they were being truthful when they said they didn't know who it was, or if they just didn't want any more conflict among our kind and lied to her to keep her from starting trouble. Margret left the pack and started out on her own. She has lived on every continent and had many lovers, both human and Were. She believes in her birthright as a royal Were and that of her children. Don't ask how many, I'm not really sure."

Mackenzie sat their completely dumbfounded. She didn't know what to say. Liam had stood and was pacing the room, looking to Mackenzie then to Geoff and would open his mouth just to close it again. Finally, he spoke.

"So, where do you come into the story?" Liam asked. He watched Geoff with trained eyes. His pacing had stopped, and his body stood rigid. Mackenzie looked between the men. She knew that neither particularly liked the other, even though just a few weeks prior they were the best of friends. She wanted to remind them of the old saying "bros before hoes," but she refused to call herself a hoe for one, and for two... what if they decided to leave her behind because she was causing too much trouble between them?

"Margret found me just after my first change when I was sixteen. I had grown up in an orphanage, and as I told Mackenzie a while ago, I had gotten a letter just before warning me of what was to come. I knew of Margret's plan to grow our number by setting a quota for each member old enough to have complete control. I knew she wanted a powerful pack. I did not know about her war on the others."

"How is it that you were her third in command, knew about *everything* else, but didn't know about her plan to force everyone into submission like her mother had? Seems like a really big blind spot, and I didn't take you for an idiot, Geoff. Well, at least not an idiot when it came to anything besides Mackenzie."

"HEY!" Mackenzie screamed out, standing from the bed. It was her turn to pace while she thought of exactly what to say. When her mind was finally made up she stood directly in front of Liam, her hand balled into fists at her side, and she could feel the anger radiating throughout her body. "What was or is between Geoff and me, is our business. Just as what was or is between you and I, is our business and I will not have either of you throwing insults at the other over me. Because by insulting him you are insulting me. Do you both understand?"

They each mumbled their agreement, and Mackenzie took a calming breath, counted her numbers backwards, and when she felt completely in control, returned to sit on the bed. "Now, ignoring our jacked up relationship status for a while, what the hell are we going to do? Find the pack of one of Rosalinda's siblings? That seems highly unlikely. I mean, they all started off in Europe, right?"

"I don't think we should look for any other pack. We become loyal to one another. We become our own pack." Liam stood as he spoke. Mackenzie knew what he was saying. He wasn't ready to trust anyone else. They could only trust one another.

"Our own pack? And who is pack leader? Who makes decisions? Who do we vow our loyalty to? Three isn't a pack. Three is just a few rogues who have nowhere to call home. We need a pack for protection, you dumb ass."

"I agree with Liam. I am not ready to trust anyone else. I mean, I thought Margret was an amazing woman who saved me and could show me how to live, and look how wrong I was about that bitch. No. We stick to just us."

"You two are going to get us killed." Geoff stormed from the room and into the bathroom, slamming the door behind him. Sighing, Mackenzie flopped back onto the bed and covered her eyes with her arm. With the light blocked out, she could almost pretend that the last few months of her life never happened. That she was in her tiny apartment just on the other side of Harvard Campus and that she had to write a paper on the mythology of ancient Europe. If only that could be true.

TWO

The morning light filtered through the dirty glass of the motel room, illuminating the bed that Mackenzie lay on. She had gone to bed alone, with both men on opposite sides of the floor. She awoke mushed between two large and hot (both temperature and physically appealing) bodies. Trying not to wake either, she moved arms and legs off her and slinked down the bed. When her feet hit the ice cold floor, she ran for the bathroom.

After a quick potty break, she started the shower. Undressing completely, she stepped under the hot spray, relishing in the feeling of getting clean after so long. As the water cascaded down her body, she took time in washing her hair and enjoyed the feeling of her fingers massaging her scalp.

Just as she had finished up, she turned the water off in time to hear two very loud screams. Apparently, the boys were awake and had found themselves sleeping in bed together. Wrapping a towel around herself, she opened the bathroom door in a fit of giggles to see both men on opposite sides of the room yelling at one another.

"You were holding me! What the hell is wrong with you?!" Liam screamed at Geoff.

"Your legs were wrapped around my hip! There is no way that my arm across your chest is worse than that! Dude, your... your... *junk* was touching my hip!"

"My junk did not! If you hadn't pulled me into you, none of this would be happening!"

Mackenzie couldn't take it anymore. She burst out in laughter so loudly both men stopped arguing to glare at her.

"This is not funny! His dick was rubbing against my thigh!"

"Oh, but it is… so funny… you… and… him… just..." Only Mackenzie couldn't actually speak in full sentences. Her words were broken up by her laughter. Neither man was laughing with her. When she finally calmed down, she added, "If you two hadn't climbed into bed with me in the middle of the night, none of it would have happened. So, it is *both* of your faults."

"Whatever, let's get dressed and go get some real food before we hoof it again." Liam shook out his annoyance as he grabbed his bag and stormed into the bathroom.

"You mean paw? Wolves don't have hooves." Geoff, having no issues with his confidence stripped down right there in front of Mackenzie. She was still wrapped in her towel, and it did not escape her attention that his eyes stayed trained on her the whole time he was in the buff. His muscles flexed, and he took his sweet time putting on a pair of boxers. By the time the fabric was actually covering him, he had to tuck his hardened length into the waistband to keep it from tenting.

Mackenzie swallowed hard. She couldn't tear her eyes away, and her body was tingling in a way that begged her to run to him and devour every inch of skin she could reach. Somehow, her self-restraint was in control instead of her hormones, and she turned from him, pulling on her under things while still covered by the towel. The skin pricked on the back of her neck, and she knew Geoff was close. He had always had that effect on her. When the warmth of his breath caressed her neck, she froze in place.

"I don't care how long it takes you to realize that I am the one for you, I won't touch you until you ask, but that doesn't mean I will make it easy on you. In fact, I think I like making it hard."

Within a second, the warmth that Geoff always brought to her was gone, but the goose bumps he left on her skin with the double innuendo was still going strong in its wake.

Breakfast at the local diner was nothing short of a spectacle. If the three werewolves could eat an entire menu on the average day, after eating next to nothing for four whole days they ate the entire menu... twice. The only problem came when Mackenzie was the only one to reach for a wallet.

"Okay, we need to fucking talk. Please tell me I am not the only one who has money. What did the two of you expect? To find a fucking money tree in the middle of the woods?"

"I didn't have anything when I moved in. Margret always supplied the cash." Liam, at least, had the sense to look a bit embarrassed with his statement. Geoff just looked annoyed.

"I've never had money. I told you, Margret found me a long ass time ago. I have a credit card through Margret, but that's it."

"So why don't you use it?" Mackenzie asked through gritted teeth.

"Do you want her to be able to find us? Have you not seen a single cop show? Credit cards are the first thing they look for when searching for people."

"But you said unless we cause trouble, she won't be looking. If I pay, that's it. No more money. Just use the damn card then cut it up. Once we get somewhere we can stay awhile, we all get jobs. All of us. None of that crap you pulled on me before, Geoff."

"Fine," Geoff huffed and threw the card on top of the bill. When the waitress came back and grabbed it, Mackenzie could feel the irritation radiating off him. The man had probably never held a real job in his life. Sure he knew responsibility being a pack leader and all, but having to deal with disgruntled customers or food preparations? Never.

"Before we head out, I need to walk around a bit. Maybe pick up a few other pieces of clothing before I destroy the card. You two can manage without me for a few hours right?"

"Why would we split up?" Mackenzie was worried. Had she pissed him off so much that he was going to try to ditch them?

"I could use a few more clothes and some other things, too. I mean, if we are going to use it, shouldn't we do it all at once so there are less transactions to follow?" Liam was watching Geoff, and his voice was hesitant, like he expected to be shut down. Which he was.

"Write down a list. I will get whatever. But seriously, after four days together, I just need some space. We can meet back up at that fast food place on the edge of town in say four hours. We can grab some burgers to take with us or something."

The waitress brought the card and the slip back waiting for the slip to be signed, and with a flick of his wrist, Geoff marked the paper with a wavy line and a decent tip. Liam quickly wrote down his list of needs and handed it off. Without another word, Geoff stood up and left.

The diner was coming to life around them, and as each group of customers filed past them in their corner booth, they took in the massive amount of dirty dishes stacked on the table. The bus boy had already made two trips and was coming back for a third.

"Time to go. No need to attract any more attention than we need to, right?" Liam scooted out of the booth and held his hand out for Mackenzie. She took it, expecting him to let go when she was firmly on her feet, but instead he laced his fingers through hers. Liam had been giving her the space she had asked for. Their connection was explosive and strong, but as badly as her body wanted to give in, she couldn't do that to him. Or to Geoff. Why did she have to keep her human sense of morals? She was a wolf, for crying out loud, and when animals got horny, they did the first thing that crossed their paths. But no. She had to be worried about sex and love and feelings and hurting someone she still cared for so deeply.

"I guess we just walk around for a while? Take in the scenery?" Mackenzie expertly extracted her hand to grab her coat that she did not really need and put it on. Her duffle bag was placed over her shoulder, and she managed to hold onto the strap with the hand that was closest to Liam. She could be close to him, hug him, even be alone with him, but holding hands was something you would do with a boyfriend. It was sweet and intimate, just not in a sexual way. She knew she needed to decide, tell them both, and just hope that when one left because she didn't pick them, it didn't tear her heart apart.

"Yeah, that works." His voice was low and when he looked her in the eyes, she saw the sadness there. He was being patient with her and not pushing her. Geoff was direct in stating exactly what he wanted, and Liam only wanted her to be happy and comfortable. There was strength in both and both still made her feel like she was flying.

~*~

Cars filled the streets and stores opened up along the main drag of town. Wherever they had wandered into was nowhere near as small the town in Montana where they had been living with the pack, but it wasn't quite a city either. It was that happy medium that so many people enjoyed.

Mackenzie expected there to be a weird tension between her and Liam as they walked, but she was pleasantly surprised. After the initial moment in the diner, Liam had slipped into the role of best friend rather easily. He would bump her shoulder with his own, point out cool things in shop windows, make comments about the idiots on the street, but never once did he cross that line from friend to love interest. If it hadn't been for the handholding in the diner, she might have even considered the fact that he was over her in that way.

Worry raced through her heart at that thought. Could she have missed her chance? What if he was the one for her? Searching his eyes for that spark, that undeniable attraction the two had between them whenever they locked eyes that held her captivated... it was still there. He was still waiting for her and she felt so relieved for a single moment that he wasn't over her. Her elation was quickly squashed when she realized how selfish she was being. She would never put up with what the two most important men in her life were putting up with, and she knew that until she couldn't resist one over the other, she wasn't going to stop.

"Look, there's a theater. Let's catch a movie, kill a few hours."

"Um, I thought we just had the money talk, Liam."

"We did. Just follow my lead."

Liam walked down the street passed the theater, then turned down an alley that looked to be used for trash pick-up. Mackenzie couldn't believe she was watching this. When she reached the alley herself, Liam was nowhere to be seen. Spinning in circles looking for him, a snicker came from behind the dumpster next to a set of stairs that led to a well-lit door.

"Liam, I swear that better be you, or when I find you, I will kick your ass for ditching me in a dirty alley!"

"Shut it, Mac. Just get back here." Sighing with relief, even though she was about to hide behind a trash can that smelled so foul her nose wrinkled and her stomach heaved, she crouched down next to Liam.

"What the hell are we doing here?" she whispered.

"Well, when that door opens, someone will come out with a bag of trash, when they do, we just make sure the door doesn't close and sneak right in. No biggie. Done it a thousand times before."

"You have done this before? You?" Mackenzie couldn't believe that. Liam was the good guy. He was the great big brother who looked after his family when his parents were working. He was the college student that worked a full time job, stayed at home, helped with homework and dishes, and cooked for his family.

"Yeah, me. I was a kid at one point too, ya know. Just… shh, look!"

Mackenzie did look. And when she did, she saw a really cute teenage boy bringing the trash out. He couldn't have been much older than sixteen. They wouldn't need to sneak at all. She had her own ways as well.

"Oh, I've got this." Mackenzie moved from behind the trash can on the opposite side of where the boy was heading. She stood off to the side, leaning against the building and watched as the tall kid approached. "Hey."

"Um, what are you doing back here? No one, but employees are allowed back here. You could get hurt." His voice cracked once or twice, and Mackenzie had to hold in a laugh at the idea of being hurt.

"Sorry, I came through that door to grab a smoke, and then realized I left my pack in my jacket in the theater and couldn't get back in. If I went around to the front they would ask for my stub, and of course, that's in my jacket, too. Do you think you could let me back in?"

She was flirting. She walked toward him with a definite sway to her hips, and she played with her hair and smiled at him. She may not have been the most physically fit girl on the planet, and never had been, but if her mother taught her one thing, it was to make what she did have as alluring as possible.

Mackenzie could see the boy swallow and hear his breath picking up as she got closer. She ignored the quiet laughter coming from behind the trash, hoping that the boy couldn't hear it either.

"I... I... I don't know," he said, keeping his eyes on her and one hand on the door, the other holding the trash bag. Mackenzie climbed the stairs and trailed a finger down his arm. A wave of goose bumps followed the path her finger had drawn, and his quickening heartbeat told her that she had won.

"I promise not to do it again. My friends are waiting for me." Then she did what she hated to do. She pouted that "feel sorry for me, I'm just a girl" pout that every annoying girl did when they really wanted to get their way. She tried not to use it, but she had to seal the deal here and quick.

"Okay, but just this once. Oh, and here," the boy tossed the trash through the air and into the open dumpster, and then pulled a pack of cigarettes out of his pocket. "Have this one. Just close the door behind you when you come in."

Mackenzie smiled triumphantly and gave him a hug. His body went rigid, and for a second, she thought maybe she squeezed too hard, maybe she had hurt him. It wouldn't have been the first time her strength got the best of her when she was trying to be nice. When she pulled back, she could see the awkward look on his face, followed by a flaming of his cheeks. Then she saw it. A tent in his pants. She looked away and pretended she never saw it.

"Thanks again, really. I bet your boss is going to wonder where you went by now, huh?" She was giving him an out, and he took it. He just nodded his head and ran in the other direction.

"Well, well, well. Mackenzie has a little vixen in her. Is that a new development, or is it just a hidden secret that only comes out to play in front of poor horny teenage boys?"

Liam had come out from his hiding spot and was watching her with humor in his eyes. Mackenzie could feel the heat filling her cheeks and knew she was blushing. She was embarrassed. It's not that she wanted to do things like that, or that she even did them all that often, but she figured it was easier than the alternative of sneaking in and being caught.

"Well, it was better than sneaking in right? Just forget it okay?"

"One lucky kid to be touched like that."

"It was his arm. Not like I grabbed his crotch or anything. Geez, he is just a kid."

"Sweetheart, any touch from you with that look you were giving him, is a lucky touch. Let's just go in before I have to watch you flirt with anyone else, okay?" His tone said he was joking, but his face looked a little weird. Could he really be jealous of a kid?

THREE

Loud explosions filled the dark room that Mackenzie and Liam had found themselves in. The large screen showed fire and cars being tossed through the air. When she looked over at Liam, he had a smile and look of awe on his face. Apparently, they had chosen a good door to sneak through.

"I think this is that new action movie I was telling you about. Come on, let's grab some seats over there." Liam pointed to the back corner of the theater. Nodding her head in agreement, Mackenzie followed behind. She was grateful for her wolfy eye sight in that moment. She couldn't even count the number of times she had tripped in a dark theater in the past, but now she could see almost as well as if the lights were on.

The fact that it was still very early in the day meant the theater was basically empty. Claiming two seats next to one another was easy. What wasn't easy was being so close to Liam in the near dark.

Mackenzie had not expected to feel her skin buzzing where they were closest. She had done so well the previous few days keeping things platonic that the surge of pure wanting took her by surprise. Goosebumps covered her skin as the hair on her arms stood upright. She shifted just slightly so that her arm rested gently against his.

Sneaking a glance in his direction, his eyes were trained on the screen, watching cars and people being blown to smithereens with a boyish grin. How soon until he could hear her rapid heartbeat? Pulling her arm away from him, Mackenzie tried to watch the movie. She tried to become entranced in the story unfolding before her, but her attention kept being pulled back to the story not being told between her and Liam.

She thought of every way to accidentally touch the man beside her. A leg graze, arms rubbing, but none of it seemed enough. Friends could hold hands. She held hands with her friends back in high school sometimes. She was so intent at trying to convince herself of this fact that she hadn't realized she had been staring at him until he looked to her questioningly.

"What?"

"Nothing. Sorry." Mackenzie tore her eyes from Liam for the second time. Not watching him was harder than watching the movie. Her fingers ached to reach out to him. His smell invaded her senses. Finally, giving in to the need in the dark theater, Mackenzie slowly moved her arm against his, grazing it ever so gently. She turned her hand until her palm lined up with his and laced their fingers together.

She could feel Liam staring at her. Hell, she could hear the air whip in her direction from the speed with which he turned his head. But she held her head steady. She would not look at him and make it any harder than she already had. She was being selfish again and she knew it, but being alone with Liam in the dark, sitting so close that her body hummed, she had to do something, and holding his hand was the least intimate thing she could think of doing.

Slowly, she felt his stare leave her and relaxed into the feeling of touching him. Tingles spread from their joined hands throughout her body until it engulfed her. Smiling, she watched the movie.

~*~

The credits rolled across the screen, and the lights slowly began to brighten. Mackenzie and Liam never did acknowledge their joined hands, and when the room was illuminated, they stood. Dreading letting go, but knowing she had to, Mackenzie pulled her hand from his to open the theater door, even though she could have very well used her other hand.

Liam reached out to reconnect them, but she didn't reciprocate. She hadn't chosen, and she didn't want to even worry about it. When they had a solid plan with a place to live, then she would deal with it. It made perfect sense to her. Plenty of people had feelings for more than one person, and they just didn't commit to anyone until they knew what they wanted. Girls back at Harvard would go on dates with different boys often before choosing one to be a couple. Her mother even encouraged her to play the field before settling down as long as she chose someone who could provide for her. That was never her intention, but thinking about it made her feel a little better about her slightly more than platonic encounters with Liam and Geoff.

She heard him sigh from behind her and guilt weighed heavy. Turning to apologize, she saw the boy from the alley come running her way. Immediately, Liam's expression changed to one of amusement as he watched her unease. She sent him a glare before turning her attention back to the boy.

"Hey! How was your movie?" The boy's voice squeaked halfway through, but he ignored it, and by the determined look on his face, he was expecting her to, as well.

"It was good. Thanks again," Mackenzie said while turning her body toward the front doors, "but I need to get going."

"Wait! Um, I mean, can I get your number?" Mackenzie cringed internally. She didn't want to make this kid think he stood a chance, because that would just be mean. But she had to let him down gently. She had enough guilt over boys coursing through her at the moment.

"I don't really have one. Just passing through. But thanks."

"Oh. Okay," the confidence in which the boy spoke was gone. His shoulders slumped, and he looked around awkwardly. "How about I give you mine, for when you are passing back through? We can grab dinner or something then."

"I don't know if I will be back through."

"I know, but take it anyway. Just in case." The boy handed her a piece of paper and gave her a soft smile before heading back over to the concession stand. Looking down at the paper, she saw that his name was Brian, and his handwriting was actually pretty good for a boy. At least, in her experience most boys had chicken scratch.

"Don't even say a word," Mackenzie growled as a laughing Liam approached. And just like that, all awkwardness between them vanished, and he teased her the whole way to the fast food place to meet up with Geoff.

Geoff leaned against the old brick building with a bag on the ground by his feet and another in his hand. As Mackenzie and Liam approached, he pushed off the wall and took two strides toward them before tossing the bag he held at Liam.

Catching it in one hand, without even flinching at the force with which the bag came barreling at him, he gave a nod of thanks. Mackenzie looked between the two men, wondering if they could ever go back to the way they were when Liam hated her and Geoff was pretending to not want her. They were friends then. Good friends. If it hadn't been for Geoff, she wasn't sure how Liam would have handled the transition to wolf. Of course, it all boiled down to Mackenzie's fault. She bit Liam. She pushed and pushed Geoff to be more than friends. She pushed Liam to accept her as his friend, until he tried to kill her and all. Then when Geoff left without so much as a word, she and Liam found they didn't hate each other. She agreed to a date to piss off Geoff which ended in feelings she never knew she was going to have. She effectively ruined a life and ended a friendship.

Perhaps she would just leave the boys on their own and find her own way. Being alone wasn't something she was unaccustomed to, as she had taken care of herself plenty of times before. She had her wolf side almost under control, and with each moon phase, she could remember more and just maybe she could control the wolf soon, too.

But then, as soon as she had thought her mind was made up, she looked to them and realized that she could never leave them. As crazy as the situation was, they were her family.

"Come on, let's get moving. I think if we can get another state over, check out the forest areas to make sure they are pack free, we can set up there for a while. We need jobs and an actual house for a while." Mackenzie smiled at Liam and Geoff who just nodded.

"Let's go. If we walk all day, sleep in whatever woods we can find tonight, and walk all day tomorrow, we should be able to cross the state line by tomorrow night." Liam had apparently picked up a map, because as he spoke, he began unfolding the large paper. He had already drawn out a few possible paths, all of which were leading toward the boarder to Washington State.

"Let's get moving then. Looks like we can probably make it to this forest by tonight, and that one by tomorrow night." Liam pointed to the map and Geoff scoffed.

"Tonight yeah, but tomorrow night we are hitting up a hotel. I pulled as much cash from the card as I could before cutting it up. Beds are essential. No more bitching about expenses. Needless to say, the card had a high cash limit."

There was no arguing with that, so Mackenzie led the way down the road. The three had fallen silent; the only sounds surrounding them were that of their feet in the slush that covered the asphalt. With the sun warming the air more each day, the cold winter's chill was fading.

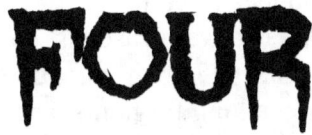

FOUR

By nightfall, Mackenzie was more than ready to make camp. As a Were, very little actually tired her out aside from the change itself, but boredom had a way of making anything tiring. She had been watching Liam and Geoff for some time, hoping they would provide entertainment, or perhaps she would think of something to talk about as they walked, but nothing ever came up.

Liam had started kicking anything that lay in his path instead of stepping over it, and if it hit something else, he would fist pump the air above him. Geoff began ripping small branches from the trees that lined the road and breaking them into little pieces, dropping them as he went. When the branch was too small for him to break any further, he would rip another from the next tree they passed. Neither looked ready to settle down for the night, both hoping to make it as far as possible to make the next day's journey that much shorter.

Mackenzie tried to find something to entertain herself. She really did. She attempted to count mile markers, how many times Liam grimaced when he kicked something too hard, and even attempted to count the stars that shone through the cloudy sky. When she damn near fell on her face she figured that was not a good idea after all.

"You guys, can we please just duck into the trees over there and sleep? I am going out of my mind here. We have been walking for hours, and its pitch black out here."

"No, it's not. At least not for us," Geoff said with a grin, "but if you want to sleep then fine. We just take fewer breaks tomorrow to make it across the border by night fall."

"We could always run tomorrow, cutting through the forest instead of taking the roads. It's not like we will tire out all that easily," Liam said as they left the road and dodged between bare tree branches and around dead stumps.

"Please, I would be at a slow jog and you two would be running full speed. But if you want to be shown up by a girl, I can get on board with that plan."

"Don't flatter yourself, Mac. I would turn before I let you out run me again. As long as I have an advantage, I am going to take it."

Geoff and Liam laughed, even though Liam himself couldn't phase on command. Mackenzie just rolled her eyes at the boys. She knew he was being a smart ass, but that didn't mean he wouldn't do it. He was still a man after all, and losing to a girl was never something they enjoyed.

"Speaking of which, how long until we can turn on command, too?" Liam asked. Mackenzie knew that Liam struggled with the fact that he had no control. He had only turned a few times and always woke up covered in blood. Thankfully, neither time was human blood.

"A while, I'm afraid. At least in my experience with bittens. First, I think you and Mac need to talk more about how to remember what is happening before you get too caught up on controlling anything. Being able to turn on command is the last element of becoming a Werewolf. You will be able to control your wolf on the full moon long before you can turn on command. And that is still years off."

"What about me? Everyone said I wouldn't be able to remember anything for at least a year or two, and I started remembering already." Mackenzie had stopped walking and looked around. They seemed to be far enough from the road, but not so deep in that finding it again would be difficult.

"I have no idea why you are different, Mac. I wish I did."

"I told Natalie and Liam how I was getting ready for the Moon, just like what you told me that first night where I got glimpses of being a wolf, and Natalie remembered more than she had been. It worked for her."

"That could have been because she was already years old, Mac. Liam, did you remember anything?"

"I wish." Liam stared hard at Mackenzie. She didn't know why he was lying, because he had told her that he had remembered a flash or two, but she didn't dare correct him. For whatever reason, he didn't want Geoff to know, and she had to respect that.

"This place is good enough. I'll be right back," Geoff turned and headed through the trees. Mackenzie didn't know what he was doing, but had a feeling she could make a few dog jokes about marking trees when he got back.

Unfortunately, he didn't come back alone or of his own free will.

~*~

Six giant men came crashing through the trees, two of which had a hold of a struggling Geoff. Jumping to their feet, Mackenzie and Liam didn't know what to do. Neither were fighters or skilled in anything except running, and they couldn't leave. They would never leave Geoff behind. At least, Mackenzie wouldn't, and Liam wouldn't leave her.

"Who are you?" Mackenzie managed to ask, even though her heart was racing with fear, and her knees were literally knocking.

"You are from the Royal Pack. You have no right to be in these woods," the biggest of the men said. He was easily almost seven feet tall and wore only a pair of torn jeans, and tribal paint coated his chest and face. They were all very similar in dress, but they ranged from tall and muscular to abnormally tall and scarily muscular. The arm of the one speaking was easily as big around as her head, and it was very tightly holding onto Geoff.

"We are not from any pack." Liam placed himself between the newcomers and Mackenzie.

"Do not lie. This Were has been here before. He came with others demanding our submission to the one who believes she is the Werewolf Destiny."

"You are right about Margret, and you might be right about Geoff being here, but we are not her pack. Geoff left them."

"Stop this foolish dribble. Grab them. Nanu will decide what to do with these trespassers."

The four others descended upon Mackenzie and Liam. Liam attempted to swing, but his fist was caught before it came even close to connecting to anyone. As the man's large fist tightened, Liam's knees buckled beneath him.

Mackenzie had learned a thing or two from her deadbeat dad before he left her and her mother when she was just a child, and decided to put it to as much use as possible.

When the smallest of the men grabbed her arm, she turned just enough to line herself up with his front. Throwing her head forward, a crunch echoed through the air, and she felt his warm blood trickle down her forehead. She knew his nose would heal in a matter of seconds, just as they all did, so before he could cope with the pain of the broken bones and heal, she brought her knee up to his balls while twisting her arm from his grasp.

While on the ground, Liam flung his feet out, catching his captor off guard and brought him to the ground where the two rolled around, both trying to gain the upper hand. Unfortunately for Liam, the other man had plenty of training and had Liam pinned to the ground in mere seconds.

Watching Liam's fight had been her detriment. The two men not injured or currently holding anyone captive grabbed her so tight she was sure that bruises were forming under their fingers on her arms. It didn't stop her, though. She would never go willingly and kicked her legs and thrashed her body as fiercely as she could.

When the man whose nuts she had crushed finally stood from the ground, he stalked to her with murder in his eyes. Mackenzie had never been more frightened in her life. For the first time since becoming a wolf, she was afraid she was going to die. The man before her could rip her heart out and leave her body there to rot and take Liam and Geoff to whoever Nanu was, and that terrified her. They could do whatever to her, but they couldn't hurt her boys.

"That was not very well thought out. Why must women make so many stupid decisions?" Before her feminist mind could respond, everything went black with a resounding crack of his fist to her temple.

Mackenzie came to before she opened her eyes. She decided to pretend to still be out of it the moment she heard Geoff's voice pleading with someone for her life. As much as she wanted to look around to see where she was and who was in charge of the asshole werewolves that held them captive, it seemed to be more in their favor if she didn't.

"I know what you think. I know that it is hard to believe I left Margret and my pack. But look at her. How hard must your man have hit her for her to still be out? I know of your pack. I know how little you think of women speaking against men, but I also know your laws concerning violence against them. Women are our lifeline as a species. Under your own laws, he must be punished. Then you may do what you must with me, with him. But let her go."

"Our pack and our laws are none of your concern. Machu will be dealt with. You do not get to demand anything. You are part of the pack that demands our submission. Our submission to a woman, no less. I do not care who her ancestors were. What the Royal Were had was demolished, and for good reason, by our forefathers. As a whole, Werewolves have flourished and grown quietly under any human radar as packs for hundreds of years. We will not submit. You may return to her and tell her that. We will fight to the death for our freedom. We are not afraid."

"We are no longer part of her pack."

"Why should I believe you? You were with the messengers."

"But I never knew the message."

Mackenzie could no longer keep quiet. Listening to their feelings on strong women should have made her keep quiet, but it only fueled her anger. Slowly, she opened her eyes to see that she, Liam, and Geoff were in the center of a circle of men. Directly in front of Geoff stood a man, the largest of them all, dressed like an Indian chief, at least what she had seen in pictures of Indian Chiefs. Mackenzie pushed up onto her hands then to her knees until she was able to stand. Geoff and Liam should not be standing alone. They were a unit. The three of them.

Liam's eyes raked over her, from top to bottom, searching her for anything that might still be wrong with her. Of course, he would find none; her body healed itself as it always would. She nodded at him once, hoping to convey that she was fine. When he gave her a small and quick smile, she knew he understood. Turning their attention back to Nanu, they stood strong.

"The woman is awake. No damage is done to her. She is Were and has healed."

"The woman has a name. The woman left the pack that you are claiming we are from for the exact reason you can't stand her. Well, maybe not entirely. I don't care that she has a vagina, but I do care that she is attacking innocent packs in some maniacal plan to take over the world. I will tell you everything I know about what she's up to, and you can let us go."

"You were trespassing and attacked my men. You will not be going anywhere." Nanu had yet to look at Mackenzie. He was directing his response to Geoff and Liam. She had reached her boiling point and moved to place herself in front of the man with only a few feet of distance between them. It was a bad idea. She knew it before she moved, but she was losing her cool.

"I was the one speaking to you. I am not from your pack. I may be a woman, but I am not insignificant. As far as you know, I am the only one who has the information you need to keep your ass safe. You think she just wants your submission to her?" Mackenzie let out a laugh. "You have no idea what that woman is up to."

"You will back away before I bring you to your knees, woman." The pure rage in Nanu's eyes, and the fact that the large circle of men surrounding them was closing in, made her pause. Her anger may be justified, but their lives were worth more than her pride.

Mackenzie held up her hands in a sign of surrender and stepped back, but not out of his line of sight. "Your men did nothing to make us believe our lives were safe. They came at us, two to one. All we did was to do what we had to do to get away. Had they told us we were on your land and had asked us to leave, we would have. But they didn't. We defended ourselves."

"This man knew our land boundaries. He has been here before, not long ago with ten others, demanding our sovereignty within six cycles of the moon. We have no intention of doing so. You may tell your pack leader she will have a fight on her hands. Perhaps we will let one of you go, with a bag of heads to give to your pack as a more convincing declaration of our decline."

"Then you will be killing in cold blood. No matter what you do to us, none of us will return to her." Mackenzie's words were calm even though her heart beat faster than a hummingbirds' wings. She knew they could all hear it, but hoped that they would pay more attention to what she actually said instead of what her body was trying to tell them.

"Mackenzie is right. None of us would return." Liam had finally spoken up. He took the steps to stand beside her, not in front of her. She was finally grateful to be treated as an equal amongst all the giant men surrounding her. She felt her whole body begin to relax, her heart slow to a more normal rhythm.

Geoff took a deep breath and stood on the other side of her. Reaching out, he grabbed her hand, lacing his fingers with hers. Mackenzie looked at him quickly. With a quick nod of his head in Liam's direction, she used her other hand to link herself to both men. The three of them stood, side by side, holding onto one another in a show of solidarity, facing down the Werewolf who would very likely end their lives.

FIVE

"You have two minutes to tell me information I need to know. If you do not, you all die. If you do, you may go." Nanu's deep voice spoke loudly. Mackenzie thought perhaps he was going to kill them anyway, but when Geoff relaxed, she wasn't so sure.

"He said it for everyone to hear. As a pack leader, your word is all you have. If we tell them anything useful, he has to let us go. Telling everyone was his word," Geoff whispered into her ear softly. He squeezed her hand and she squeezed Liam's. Looking to her right, she saw the confusion on his face that had to be on hers just moments before. She gave him what she hoped was a reassuring glance, before turning her attention back to Nanu.

"Two minutes is all I need," Geoff said.

"Not you. Her," Nanu dismissed Geoff with a wave of his hand but kept his eyes on Mackenzie. "I have no trust in you. Her. She speaks up out of love and stupidity. Women are not meant to be heard, but she would rather die than see the two of you fall before her. She will be honest to keep you alive. Grab them!"

And just like that, Mackenzie was left standing alone in front of Nanu. Geoff and Liam were held by the neck on their knees. Right before her eyes, two more of the pack members changed, their backs arching and their heads twisting in angles that were simply not possible for a human, and the sound of every bone breaking then resetting filled the air for all of ten seconds. When silence filled the air, two very large wolves stood before her, baring teeth and growling. Their paws thundered as they hit the ground, pacing in front of her.

"Speak or they lose their heads." Nanu flicked his hand and the wolves placed themselves in front of the two people Mackenzie loved most in the world.

"Margret thinks she is meant to rule all werewolves all over the world. Her Mother ruled before there were packs, and her mother before her. She is next in line, and because she was just a girl when her mother was killed by her father, her Aunts decided it was best left up to each family or pack to keep their own safe."

"We do not need a history lesson. I was a boy when that happened. This is not useful information." The two wolves leapt at Liam and Geoff, biting down hard on their arms. The men screamed out in pain, and the watching circle of Nanu's pack cheered.

"WAIT! I know more!" Once again, Nanu waived his hand, and the wolves released them, but not moving farther back than a foot, still openly growling, blood coating their muzzles. "Her pack is big and gets bigger with each cycle. She makes each member turn humans to increase their size. They have three houses, in three different states. They just acquired another large pack in California. Her power is growing."

Nanu said nothing. He stared at her as if he were trying to figure out how much more she had to tell. The honest answer was not much. She knew that Margret planned on attacking pack after pack, and killing the pack leader no matter if they surrendered or not. She knew that she was targeting specific humans but had no real clue why. She knew that Margret was an evil woman who put on the facade of a caring mother.

"How many packs has she taken?"

"I don't know. I just know about the one. I was bitten just five months ago. In that time, there have been three humans turned and added to her ranks, and one pack taken over. She won't stop until she has everyone, either by loyalty or by death."

"You are bitten?" The sheer look of disgust on his face was enough to send ripples of self-doubt through her. He turned his back on her and walked away. "Let them go. Never return."

~*~

Liam and Geoff stood; the pack surrounding them turned their backs. The torn flesh on the men's arms had already begun to knit itself back together as they took shaky steps toward Mackenzie. Once they were by her side, their strength had almost fully returned as the wounds were now healed and their bodies were already beginning to replace the blood that had been lost.

"Which way gets us as far from their land as quickly as possible?" Liam muttered under his breath.

"This way." Geoff charged ahead of them. Mackenzie followed silently, refusing to look over her shoulder at the pack behind her. Liam's strides matched Mackenzie's, step by step, never leaving her side, shooting daggers from his eyes at the back of Geoff's head. "Just another hour or so, and we should be in the clear."

"Into another packs domain?" Liam asked with a sneer. He was angry, and he had every right to be. They had all trusted in Geoff's knowledge of the surrounding area, and to find out that he had, in fact, been exactly there, threatening another packs land just months prior, was a slap in the face.

"Not now. Let's save our heads by getting the fuck out of here first, then you can bitch, okay?" Geoff had turned and seethed his words at Liam. Mackenzie knew there would be tension, and almost being killed hadn't helped matters. She had to come up with a way to smooth things over between the two and fast.

"Will you both just chill out? Better idea, let's run and cut the hour or so in half. *Then* you can argue all you want." Mackenzie didn't wait for either man to respond. She shoved past Geoff and took off in a run. She just hoped she was going the right way.

~*~

Mackenzie had been right as Geoff called out that they were in the clear after only forty minutes. She enjoyed her time alone, even if it was running through trees and jumping over fallen logs. She missed running just for the fun of it. It had been almost a week since her last run, and even though the boys were behind her, the space to be alone had given her time to think.

Mackenzie slowed down and stopped near a small brook that cut through the trees. Mackenzie smiled seeing the running water. The ice had started melting, and with the water running, it meant that spring was on its way.

Liam and Geoff caught up moments later. Mackenzie smiled at the fact that she was faster than both of them. She may not be a born were and able to control everything about her change like Geoff, and she may not be as emotionally stable as Liam, but she was fast.

"Okay, we ran. We left that pack's land. Now explain what the fuck we were doing there if you knew they were hostile?" Liam watched Geoff with a careful eye. It was obvious that he didn't trust him, and Mackenzie wasn't sure how to fix that. Was she being blind because of her feelings, and her body's reaction to Geoff?

"Yes, I knew it was there land. I didn't think we would be caught, because I had kept us on the outside perimeter. And I didn't know that Margret had demanded their alliance. We have already gone over this. I wasn't in on her plans. I had been told we were being attacked because of who she was. Because of the fact that her mother *was* the leader of all werewolves, born and bitten. If our kind returned to the way of monarchy, she would be the rightful leader due to her lineage, just as human kings and queens do it. I had been told they were attacking us to make sure that never happened. To take her out because they feared what could happen, but never would. I didn't know."

"Then why did Nanu think you did. You were on that message mission, weren't you?" Liam had stood and was pacing back and forth. His words were much calmer than before, but skepticism was still obvious in his tone.

"I was, but I wasn't privy to the message itself. I had been told that we were making rounds to inform everyone that the rumors were false. I had also been told to let Mason handle the communication because I can be intimidating. He was the one who spoke with the pack leaders. Not me."

"Mason? I didn't realize he had a place on whatever kind of council thing Margret was talking about." Mackenzie had finally joined the conversation. She had been listening to the boys long enough. Margret had offered Mackenzie a place on the council for being such an extraordinary Were. A privilege apparently. Mackenzie had been targeted to be changed, because Margret had seen something in her as a human that told her she would be a potentially amazing Werewolf. If only she had been given an option.

"He does. I had thought he was directly below my position, but apparently I was wrong. I was lead to believe that, but if he knew more than I did, there is no doubt that she was using me for some reason. I just don't know what."

"Are we on some other pack's land now? One that you visited before?" Liam had stopped his pacing and stood with his arms crossed.

"Of course we are. There isn't one inch of land that isn't claimed. If you want to take land for yourself you fight for it. Or you stick to the city, and even some of those are taken. But these wolves are very passive. They only monitor their land when it's close to a moon cycle. We have at least a few weeks before anyone will bother us."

"Alright. Let's just get some sleep."

Mackenzie walked over to Liam, placed a hand on his arm and squeezed. With a nod of her head to the side, she let him know she wanted him to follow. Geoff took notice of the two, and if she wasn't mistaken, saw a fire light in his eyes when she walked off with Liam. Sighing, she knew she would have to explain things to him later.

She really wished she didn't have feelings for them both, no matter how hard she tried to shut them off. Neither man deserved to be kept on the hook waiting for her to choose, but she was too selfish to let them both go.

"What is it?" Liam asked when they were far enough away that whispered voices would be kept private from Werewolf hearing. He had turned his body to hers and began rubbing his hands up and down her arms.

"I know the last few days have gone anything but smooth, but we need to stick together and not fight within our group. I almost lost you today. That was the scariest thing I have ever had to live through. Worse than my own change. Worse than watching you change because of what I did. The two of you, both of you, are so damn important to me, and I don't know what I would do without you. Please, can we try to get along?"

Mackenzie was staring into his eyes during her entire speech. She tried to ignore the tingles that his caressing hands left in their wake. She tried to ignore the pounding of her heart whenever the two of them were that close. She tried to ignore the hunger for her in his stare.

"For you, I will bite my tongue, but I don't trust him. I will do whatever I have to do to keep you safe."

"Thank you."

Liam took a step forward, pulling her into his arms. Mackenzie sunk into his warmth and relished in the feeling that filled her when she was close to him.

SIX

The next day and the day after that, and even the day after that, were filled with silence between the men and awkward conversations that Mackenzie tried to start to fill the void. The change in direction after the run in with Nanu's pack had sent them deeper into the forests and farther from any kind of real civilization.

"Give me your knife." Liam stood in front of Geoff with his hand out. Asking for a weapon wasn't what anyone expected to be the first thing he said to him, and both Geoff and Mackenzie looked at him with skepticism. "I'm hungry, we ran out of cold burgers days ago, and we don't even know exactly where we are or when we will be close to human civilization to buy food, so one of us needs to hunt. I'm pretty sure I'm the only one who can do it without being a wolf, so give me your knife."

"You hunt?" Mackenzie asked. For whatever reason, that was a real turn on for her. He was going to take a knife and go into the woods and come back with food for them all that wasn't mangled and covered in wolf drool.

"Yeah, my Dad and I used to go all the time. I typically had a gun, but we did do small animals every once in a while with traps and knives."

"Alright. Sounds good to me. Just try not to lose the knife, okay?" Geoff handed over his large buck knife and turned back to the fire he was attempting to build. The longer they traveled, the dryer the trees and fallen branches were. Mackenzie thought that they must be headed south, escaping the winter weather and finding dryer land.

Liam gave her a smile before disappearing into the forest. Smiling back, despite the fact that he had already disappeared, she sighed.

"Fire's ready." Turning around Mackenzie found Geoff relaxing against a large boulder next to a big fire. He had cleared a large circle and dug a pit, surrounding it with small stones, before filling it with twigs and branches and setting it ablaze.

"Very nice. We'll be able to cook whatever Liam brings back."

"Right. Come sit with me. We haven't really had any time, you and me." Mackenzie knew that was true. She didn't trust herself alone with either man. With her emotions on high since she turned, and the way they both made her feel, it was safer not to be. Not to mention, she really didn't have the opportunity. The movies with Liam was as close as she got, and it took all of her will power not to jump him right there. "I won't bite, promise."

Mackenzie laughed when she looked to him and saw his grin. He knew she liked it when he bit her, and the memories of their small amount of time together flooded her. Slowly, she made her way to him, sitting down but making sure that they didn't touch anywhere. Geoff watched her with one eyebrow raised as if to say "are you kidding me" then reached out, wrapped his arm around her shoulders and pulled her body flush against his side.

Mackenzie snuggled in to Geoff, allowing herself to relish in their closeness. If only she could close her eyes and pretend that everything was okay. That she and Geoff had hit it off right away, and that he never tried to keep her at arms-length, that she had never turned Liam… because then the moment she found herself in could be completely perfect.

But those things had happened.

"Do you ever wonder where we would be if I wasn't such an idiot when we first met? If I had said to just screw the rules and had just taken what I wanted? I kept saying we had to be sure of what we wanted because of the mating rules of our kind, but what if they are all wrong?"

Taking a minute to think about what he just said Mackenzie watched the fire crackle and dance in the pit. She wanted to agree to everything he just said, because it was true. It was exactly what she was thinking, but that didn't mean it was a road they should go down.

"Of course I have, but we can't change what happened any more than we can predict our future. Let's just worry about right now."

"Right now is good. Better than it's been in a while." Geoff leaned over and ran his nose along her neck and jaw, inhaling deeply. Shivers ran down Mackenzie's spine when the scruff on his face scratched along her skin. Tilting her head away from him, she opened her neck up to more of his attention.

"You believe me, right?" Geoff asked between nips of her skin and soft kisses to soothe the sting afterward. She had almost missed his question entirely, but his affection stopped, and he stared at her, waiting for an answer.

"I do." And she did. Most of the time. She hated that there were times when she just thought the coincidences were too large to be believable. But when she looked in his eyes and saw the way he looked at her, she knew that he wouldn't hurt her. She had to believe him. He couldn't be the type of person that Margret was.

"Liam doesn't. I'm just not sure if that has more to do with me or you."

"Let's not talk about this, okay? He trusts me, and I trust you. He'll come around."

"Okay. Let's not talk at all then." Geoff began caressing her arm again, and she smiled to herself. She knew he wouldn't be able to stay away.

"What happened to the hotel being the last time you would touch me first?"

"Come on, we both knew that wasn't going to happen." Geoff laughed as he kissed her temple, then the tip of her ear, her jaw, and just as he was turning her by the chin to cover her lips with his, a rustle in the trees alerted them to the fact that they were not actually alone.

Mackenzie pulled away, not wanting Liam to walk in and see the two of them so close, let alone kissing. It wouldn't be right, and it would hurt him. Just as she had pulled her hand from Liam's, in order to keep Geoff from seeing their intimacy to protect his feelings. Knowing that no matter what she did was hurting someone, the guilt raked through her. Mackenzie couldn't look at Geoff, and when Liam finally appeared through the trees, she couldn't look at him either.

"Caught two rabbits. It's not much, but it's something."

"Great, do you happen to know how to butcher them, too? Or are we supposed to throw them in the fire fur and all?" Geoff's acidic tone didn't go unnoticed. Liam instantly went on the defensive, and Mackenzie was caught in the middle.

"Oh, so the great Werewolf who has lived since before electricity and stoves doesn't know how to butcher an animal? Very impressive." Liam rolled his eyes and turned his back, preparing to clean the rabbits on a nearby rock.

"More impressive than you. If Mackenzie hadn't have bitten you and linked the two of you through the sire bond, there would be nothing interesting about your relationship with her. Must really piss you off that the only reason you even have a glimmer of a chance with her is that her DNA is running through yours."

Geoff had stood and his whole body was tense, ready to strike. Mackenzie didn't know what had changed the current between the two, or why Geoff chose that moment to bring up the giant elephant in the room, so to speak, but he had, and it didn't look like it was going to end pleasantly.

Liam turned to face Geoff, the knife still clutched in his hand, his knuckles turning white from the pressure with which he held it. His normally friendly and light eyes turned steely and murderous. Mackenzie watched both men, hoping neither would actually strike.

"Right, because pushing her away at every turn was guaranteeing you a place in her heart. Lying to her about everything is the perfect way to build a relationship. The fact is, if Mackenzie and I had met while we were both still human, we would still have fallen for each other."

"Fallen for each other? Are you daft? If she had fallen for you, you would be together, and I wouldn't matter. The fact is, she turned to you to make me jealous, and then when I came back, she realized she couldn't let me go. Only she can't let you go either. She feels the sire bond as much as you do and hurting you hurts her."

"HELLO! Do either of you care that I am standing right here?" Mackenzie had moved beyond worried about the two and straight into pissed off.

"She and I sure as hell have a lot more in common than the two of you. What is there for you? A physical attraction that you weren't even willing to give in to until you found out that I was more than willing? You didn't want her, but you didn't want anyone else to have her either. It's the only reason you changed your tune. If I hadn't been interested, neither would you, and that is the stupidest thing you could do. The problem is she knows it. She knows that you don't really want her. At least deep down she does. Otherwise, she would have gone with you in a heartbeat. But she knows you are going to hurt her, and she knows I never would."

"SERIOUSLY STANDING RIGHT FUCKING HERE!" Mackenzie now yelled at the top of her lungs. When the men still squared off ignoring her, she did the only thing she could think of. She picked up two rocks and threw them directly at their fucking heads.

Each rock hit its target, and the groan that left both men put a satisfied smile on her face. When they both turned in her direction, she started speaking, not giving them a chance to say a word.

"I know the two of you turn into giant fucking dogs and all, but I am not a tree to piss on. I will not be claimed. I will not be argued about right in fucking front of me and ignored. At this point, I am close to saying forget it with both of you and going my own damn way. I don't want to, but I cannot handle the tension between everyone. Fucking hell, I am going out of my damn mind! Can we please just figure out what the hell we are doing, where we are going, and how we are going to make it as a pack of three before having to deal with any of the romance crap? Yes, I have chemistry with you both. Yes, all of us are a bit on edge, and as adults we can admit to sexual tension out the damn wazoo, but Jesus Christ, can we not label *anything* yet?"

Both men stood in silence and just watched her. When she realized that they weren't going to actually say anything, she took the knife from Liam and walked over to the rock the rabbits were laying on.

She knew how to clean game meat. She didn't go hunting with her father or any of her mother's boyfriends, but she did know how to clean and cook what they brought home.

~*~

Mackenzie cleaned and cooked their meal without any further acknowledgement of the men. The only noises that filled the air were that of the local wild life and the crackling fire. She saw Liam attempt to talk a few times, but close his mouth quickly before words came out. Geoff, on the other hand, was sulking. He decided not to even attempt to make small talk and just pout against a tree on the other side of the fire from the other two. She was perfectly happy with this. If he wanted to pout like a child, he could sit in time out like a child.

After an hour, the silence started getting to her, though. It was beginning to feel worse than when the boys were trying to decode her every move. Before she could say anything, Geoff jumped to his feet and faced the opposite direction. Both Liam and

Mackenzie watched him, and then a fast-paced footfall sounded from the trees, followed by cracks of twigs and whips of branches being pushed out of the way.

"Get ready!" Geoff called before ripping his clothing from his body and changing into his wolf. Mackenzie and Liam stood there, watching and waiting, wishing they too had the advantage of turning into their wolves. What had once been what they wished would never occur again, could now be the only thing to keep them alive in an even fight.

Geoff's hackles were raised, and a growl began to erupt from his very large body. Then, out of nowhere, another wolf jumped out from the trees, jaws wide open and dark fur flying as it landed on top of wolf-Geoff. Mackenzie and Liam watched the two beasts snapping and wrestling with one another on the ground.

When another man came through the trees and jumped at Liam, Mackenzie was in shock. The two men and the two wolves fought. Mackenzie was just glad that the man fighting Liam wasn't in wolf form. They would be dead in seconds if another born had come along and had been able to turn on command. Mackenzie picked up one of the rocks she had thrown at the boys earlier and chucked it at the stranger's head. It was risky, because she could have hit Liam, but had hope that he would see what she was doing and keep the man's back to her long enough for the stone to make contact.

A howl pierced through the growls and groans being made by all those around her, and Mackenzie whipped around, prepared to see the worst. The strange wolf was atop of wolf-Geoff, and its teeth were bared just inches from his neck. She had no time to think. Mackenzie launched herself onto the back of the Werewolf.

Wrapping one arm around its neck to hold on as it whipped her back and forth, she used her other hand to blind it. Her fingers found the moistest area and dug in, the blood oozing down her hand, as the wolf howled in pain.

She could feel the fibers of the wolf's eye trying to mend itself around her finger, so she pulled it out just enough to shove it back through. When wolf-Geoff had finally stood and growled at her, she took it as a sign to get the hell out of there before the wolf she was currently sitting astride like a bucking bronco decided to make her its next meal.

Mackenzie pulled her fingers from its eye socket once again and released its neck and allowed the wolf's whipping motion to throw her from its body. Landing against a tree hurt like hell, but she knew if she had just tried to jump off and run, she would be dead.

Wolf-Geoff had pinned the half blind wolf to the ground and bit down on its throat in a quick strike. Blood poured from the wolf's neck, soaking the ground. Wolf-Geoff went in for the kill, and Mackenzie had to look away.

When she did, she saw that Liam sat atop his attacker as well, his hands to his throat. The man's whole face was blue, but they both knew the minute he let go, their Werewolf body would heal them in minutes, if not seconds, and the fight would only continue.

Wolf-Geoff walked over to Liam, covered in blood, and nudged his shoulder. Looking at the two of them, Mackenzie could finally see that while they were very different, they were still very much the same.

Liam moved and wolf-Geoff finished off the attacker just as he had the Werewolf behind them.

~*~

"Are you fucking crazy, Mackenzie?" Geoff screamed at her after turning back to his human form. He used his shirt to wipe the blood from his body. He was vibrating with anger, that much she could tell, but she didn't understand why he was so angry with her.

"What the hell did I do?"

"What did you do? Are you fucking kidding me? Liam, a little help here?" Liam had been going through the pockets of the dead man when he looked up and glared at her. She knew she had wished they would get along more, but she didn't mean for them to gang up on her, especially on something she didn't even understand.

"You could have gotten yourself killed. That's what you did. You should have let us handle it."

"You two are the insane ones. If I hadn't have jumped in, who knows if either of you would even be alive right now! Geoff, that damn wolf almost ripped your head off before I blinded him, and Liam, what would you have done without that asshole being blindsided by a rock to the back of his fucking head? I am not some little girl that needs protecting!"

"You are strong in your own right. You are capable of thinking on your feet, and yes, that is very helpful in situations like that. But had it gone wrong, had you ended up getting yourself killed trying to save one of us, neither would be able to live with that, Mac." Geoff's voice had softened, and Liam just stood there, not saying a word.

"And how do you think I would feel if I did nothing and you died?"

"I think Geoff should spend some time training us. Getting us up to speed on the style of fighting we are going to need to go against these people."

"What people?"

Liam held up a little card. When Geoff took it from him and read what it said, he cursed and threw it so hard at a tree that it lodged itself in the bark. Mackenzie ran over and pulled the plastic ID card out, reading the name and address on the card. His name was John Barret and he lived in the California pack house. Margret had sent assassins after them.

SEVEN

Mackenzie stood watching the dead wolf's body for ages. Geoff and Liam were disposing of the other body, and all she could do was stare at the headless wolf lying in a puddle of blood. She wasn't sure what she expected to see. It wasn't going to heal, she knew that much. Maybe it would turn back into its human form, and she could see whom it was that had turned against them. Or did the whole pack view it as they were the ones who were in the wrong? Were they considered the bad guys to the people who had once been family?

"A little help over here?" Geoff's voice startled her from her thoughts. Tearing her eyes away from the dead wolf in front of her, she saw the body of a headless man being tossed into a hole.

"Right, what do you need me to do?" Mackenzie walked over to where Geoff stood caked in blood and mud.

"Find the head?" Bile rose in her throat, but she quickly swallowed it down. The boys already saw her as someone to protect, she didn't need to add squeamish to the list. Nodding in agreement, she slowly walked along the area keeping her eyes to the ground for the missing head.

Looking up for just a moment to check on the boys, she saw them once again as they worked together to dig another whole for the wolf body. She was glad they were finally getting along again. Too bad they had to bond over dead bodies and graves.

Her foot stepped into something warm and wet, soaking through the top of her sock and into her shoe. A mumble of irritation seeped from her until she looked down and let out a disgusted scream. She had managed to step directly *into* the head.

Liam raced to her side to hold her steady as Geoff pulled it from her foot with a loud and wet slurping noise as it went.

"Well, you found it." Geoff was trying to hide a laugh behind his words, and Liam began coughing to cover his own reaction to her miss-step.

"Shut up, and get rid of it." Mackenzie wasn't laughing. She was pissed and needed to let it out. Storming away from them, she approached a large tree surrounded by rocks and fallen branches. One by one, she picked each limb up and hit the trunk as hard as she could as she sent splinters of wood flying. With every swing she screamed out in frustration. If there was anyone else anywhere in the vicinity, they knew exactly where she was. Was it a good idea when they were apparently being hunted by those who had called them family just weeks before? No. But did it make her feel better? Absolutely.

When the branches were gone, she stared on the rocks, throwing them as hard as she possibly could into the tree, past the tree, into the air. It didn't matter where as long as she threw it as hard and as fast as her arms would allow. When the rocks were gone, she started punching the tree, feeling her skin rip open and heal over and over again. When she heard a snap of her thumb bone and the tingling of it trying to heal, but never quite managing because she kept going even then, Liam came and wrapped his arms around her, holding her still.

Standing still while her body healed itself was hard. She just wanted to keep going, keep destroying whatever she could. Then, as if she had never been angry in the first place, the rage left her. She hadn't had a mood swing like that since the first month or two after her change, and it scared her. She had thought she had come so far, but she had no control, she couldn't even stop when she broke her hand and didn't allow it to heal. Liam had to stop her.

Slowly, a smile came to her face. Liam stopped her. She had no anger toward him. She didn't turn and take it out on him. She could have and had in the past with others who got in the way of her and whatever she was actively destroying, but not this time. Either she was getting more control even with her anger, or it was just Liam. Even when on a rampage she couldn't hurt him.

"Mac? Can Liam let you go? Are you better now?" Geoff had moved to stand in front of her, and the concern in his dark eyes was evident. His brows were scrunched and his eyes were searching hers. When he reached out and began rubbing her arms up and down, she sighed. She was better. The two of them, both of them, had made sure of that.

Nodding, Liam let her go. When she didn't attack either of them, they stepped back, their relief evident.

"Let me see your hand. The bone healed already, but we need to make sure it healed in place or we will have to rebreak it so it can set right." Geoff held his hand out, and she placed her no longer injured hand in his. "Good, it set just fine. But I think it's about time for some fighting refreshers. You shouldn't have had your thumb in the way. I thought you said your Dad taught you to fight?"

"Yeah, he did, when I was like eight. And he taught me about fighting against people my own size, not trees."

"Got it. Human girl fighting against human girls. Not trees. Well, we will have to fix that. Starting tomorrow, I'll train you both in fighting with another being that heals as fast as you do."

"What about turning? Can we learn to do that sooner, too?"

"I've never seen it done, but I've also never seen a bitten just months into their new lives remember their phases, either."

~*~

"AGAIN!" Geoff bellowed at Mackenzie and Liam. They had been grappling for hours. And for days upon days upon days before that. Fighting with Weres was less about punching and more about wrestling them to the ground. Whatever it took to get their throats in a vulnerable position.

Mackenzie lunged at Liam. At first, neither had been too sure about fighting the other without holding back, but now Mackenzie looked forward to it. She felt free when she let go of her inhibitions and to fight like a wolf. Geoff had told her not to hold anything back. Put every ounce of feeling she had for anything into every move she used in a fight, and she was sure to prevail.

The problem with that was he told Liam the same thing. When Liam stopped holding back, Mackenzie had a very hard time beating him. In fact, she hadn't beaten him once, and it was pissing her off.

Liam quickly took the upper hand and tackled her to the ground, positioning himself above her with one knee between her legs, one arm holding both of her hands above her head and his other hand at her throat.

"FUCK!" she screamed, jerking her body back and forth. When a sly smile spread on his face when her attempt to get away failed, she brought her knee up as fast and as hard as she could in the direction of his dick. She might not be at the best angle, but she sure as hell was going to try.

Liam's face contorted in pain when her knee connected with him. Taking the only advantage she had, she flipped them, and just as she thought she was going to win the match, his pain turned to anger and he spun them yet again, but stood holding her by her shoulders and slammed her into a tree.

"ENOUGH!" Geoff called, walking toward them as if nothing unusual had occurred. "Much better, Mac. Always take any opportunity given to you. There is no such thing as fighting dirty when you are going against someone twice your size and skill. Survival is the only important thing."

"Liam, good recovery. How are the balls?"

Liam had let Mac down and was visibly shaking, trying to get control of himself again. Mackenzie knew exactly what he was doing because she too was trying to get herself back. Letting go of all inhibitions and giving into the wolf was not easy to come back from. When she had her mind and emotions back, guilt flooded through her for kneeing him in his manly bits. She hoped that the healing Werewolf blood worked everywhere, and she didn't do any permanent damage.

"Fine." Liam's one word answer, followed by his retreat into the woods, told her that he wasn't able to come back to himself as quickly as she had, or perhaps he didn't care that they were grappling and thought the ball blow was not okay. She wouldn't blame him, a man and his balls had a certain relationship, after all. At least that's what she thought after listening to college frat boys for the first and only few months of her Harvard experience.

If Mackenzie were still in school, she would be three months from the end of her first year. But she wasn't and dwelling on that, would get her nowhere, but depression, and they hadn't seen a store or road in well over a week, so a chocolate fix would be impossible.

"He'll calm down. Just give him a few minutes." Geoff's words were comforting if not a bit confusing. Liam hadn't reacted this way after a session before.

"How do you know? Did I go too far?"

"No, when I called an end he 'woke' from the fight to find himself in a position that he had no control over. He would have ripped into your neck in another few moments, and the fact that he could do that to you scared him. He normally holds back, just enough to make sure to never lose control and hurt you for real. His body took over his mind, and he was in full Werewolf mentality at the end there."

"Oh." Mackenzie wasn't sure what to do with that information. Not only had he always been holding back, and she was still losing, but also if Geoff hadn't been there, she would have been a goner, or at least seriously hurt. Geoff stepped forward and wrapped her in his arms and held her. It was exactly what she needed, comfort and support and nothing more.

Realizing that she was even farther from holding her own in a fight just solidified her resolve to learn to force the change whenever she needed. If she was in a fight, and she was getting her ass kicked, she would channel her wolf, and she would be the one with the upper hand. At least, that was how she tried to explain it to Geoff.

"Mac, I get that you're worried, I do. But you haven't even been a Were for a full year. Trying to teach you to change isn't going to make a damn bit of difference. It will just piss you off when you can't do it."

"But you don't know that I can't! Just tell me how you teach the others, and I will try on my own. You can keep working with Liam on the hand-to-hand thing, and I can do something that I might actually be good at. We already know that, for some reason, my wolfy side is faster than it should be and that my brain is tempering faster than normal, too. Let me try."

"You are the one who needs more hand-to-hand practice. Why in the hell would you want to hinder your skills even more by not practicing?"

"Because, Liam is holding back because of me. Maybe if you send him after a tree, or grapple with him yourself, he will let go and do the best he can."

"No."

"No? That's it? Just no?"

"Just no. We need to get back to work. We have less than a week until the moon cycle, and we need to keep going. We need to find a place of our own."

"I thought you said there was no place to call our own, packs basically already had all of the country."

"There are a few packs that would let a small pack of three onto their land without incident. We just need to get established. A house, a shower, a fucking bed. I don't know about you, but I'm done with the woods."

"Fine, you go back to working with Liam, I will work on convincing my body to change, and after the cycle, we find a place to live for good."

"Mac, I said no."

"Geoff, you said no to teaching me yourself. Fine. You don't have to. I will figure it out on my own. You do not get to tell me what to do."

"Why are you so damn stubborn?"

"Why are you?"

Geoff growled his frustration before turning and walking away from her. He could be mad all he wanted, but she was going to find a way to protect herself, and them, if it was the last thing she did. She learned all the moves that Liam had, but she wasn't strong enough to execute them, and while she was smart, she couldn't see three moves ahead as he could, either. Perhaps he was a skilled fighter, and if they are attacked again, she will be able to hold her own, but that wasn't something she was willing to risk.

When she trained her brain into accelerating her memory of her time as a wolf, and even when she was able to get one single command to her wolf, it had all started with her spending the day thinking about what she loved as a human. Her human memories of love and happiness.

Mackenzie left the boys behind as she walked to a clearing that she had found the day before. Trees completely surrounded it, almost like a solid fence with very little space between them. The ground was soggy, but the snow had all melted. If there had even been any snow where they were at all. With all the traveling they had been doing, the area might not even be one that sees any of the white fluff in the winter. Grass had begun to spring up sporadically around the area, and the sun, high in the sky, was warming the area nicely. The trees blocked any wind, and without a single cloud in the sky, the sun's light was able to warm her without the chill that normally accompanied early March.

Breathing in deeply, the woodsy scent filled her nose. It was all she had smelled in weeks, and for the first time since she became a Were, she didn't have the intense pull to nature. She was living in it. Geoff was so eager to be back in a house and only going to the woods when they needed to, but she had no urge for a house. No urge to be cooped up and away from the natural world. Would a hot shower be nice? Absolutely. There were things about living in a house that she would welcome should the option arise, like a hot shower and perhaps a soft bed, but sleeping under the stars, with the sounds of the woods, and the sense of calm would trump all of that every time.

Mackenzie slowly began taking her clothing off. As each piece hit the ground, she felt her connection to the world around her grow. When she was completely bare, she closed her eyes and lived in her mind. Her mother, grandmother, even times with her father. Geoff and Liam.

"Just let it go. Let go of this body." Mackenzie was talking out loud ever so softly to herself, urging her body to make the change. But it didn't.

Screaming in frustration, she heard the rapid footfalls of Geoff and Liam. Quickly grabbing her shirt and slipping it over her head, she covered herself just before they broke through the trees.

"I'm fine."

"What was that about?"

"Nothing, I said I'm fine. Now go."

Both men looked at her as if she had lost her mind, but did as she asked. They did this every day for the next four days.

The full moon was rising in the sky and both men were standing around with her, waiting for the moment the moon hit the highest point in the sky and bathed them in its light to force their bodies into the change.

Mackenzie hadn't given up. She was still determined to cause the change herself. With the moon full and the forced change imminent, she could feel her body trying to give in to her will. Then, every time she thought of her human life, the love, everything that helped her keep part of her brain in control, the feeling would fade.

As if a light switch had flicked on, she realized to turn on command wasn't about embracing her human nature; it was about embracing her wolf. Every thought was gone. She dug her toes into the ground beneath her, reached her arms out into the night sky, and allowed every animalistic urge and thought she ever fought off to come to the surface of her mind.

She watched the moon ascend above the trees, and then dropped to the ground with a loud crack and she turned. Before either man did.

EIGHT

She watches as the two wolves stood before her in the glow of the moonlight. Their yellow-green eyes all piercing through the darkness as the glow reflects back into the world. A small growl erupts from the snow white wolf and Mackenzie-wolf returns the sentiment. As the growl passes through her mouth, her teeth are bared as she, too, backs away from the others. For whatever reason, the black wolf just stood there, watching her.

As soon as she felt safe enough, she turned on all four and charged off into the night. Her hunger so apparent that anything with a heartbeat sent her charging. Her marble colored fur turning blacker with each hunt, and as she tended to roll around once she caught her prey. Playing with her meal before killing and devouring it seemed to entertain her.

A snapped twig and the scent of another predator, but a familiar scent, alerted her to the presence of another. Lifting her head slowly, careful to not make a sound, her ears twitched, listening for the intruder. Blood humming beneath her skin, she suddenly felt at ease. A flash of white cut across the dark path that lay in front of her, yet she did not move. Watching and waiting, she listened. The thrum of its heart, the heavy pants of its breath, the thud of its paws against the moist ground. It was coming closer but instead of being ready to attack, she sat and waited.

Something told her that the white wolf was no enemy. She knew deep down that her blood was vibrating with anticipation but not fear. There was a distinct difference between fear, and whatever she was feeling then. As if she knew she was being watched, she turned her head to the right, sniffing the air with her muzzle pointing upward, and then letting out a playful bark.

Slowly she lowered her front to the ground and raised her hind quarters in the air. For added measure a swish of her tail, ensuring that the newcomer knew her intentions were not of ill will.

The white wolf broke through the trees slowly, as if not sure what to make of her. She waited as it slowly padded toward her before mimicking her stance, tail wagging, and all. Both wolves ran at each other and began playfully nipping and wrestling with one another.

A howl broke through the trees, full of sorrow and longing. They both stopped momentarily, the white wolf perched on top of her and pinning her to the ground to listen to the night sky and return the sad wolf's call. She had hope that he would feel a part of something greater than himself when he heard the return. The growl that erupted from the sidelines of her and the white wolf's play are followed immediately by a very large black wolf charging through and tackling the white wolf from atop her.

Immediately on high alert, she charged at the mass of fur and teeth wrestling before her. Were they too playing? Or had the black wolf attacked? Half the noises from them sounded harsh but the other half sounded much like her own just moments before. She almost jumped into the mix of the two large wolves, but became distracted by the scent of prey.

She knew the others would smell it soon, and it was hers. She charged off without a second glance at the black and white wolves behind her. The further she got from them, the hum in her veins quieted. Pushed further by her hunger and the scent of whatever was emitting that delicious metallic blood scent just a little ways away, she forgot about everything else.

Just ahead a statuesque deer with antlers almost as large as the animal itself stood nibbling the new growth on the ground. She could see the subtle rise and fall pulse of blood coursing through its neck just under its hide. Salivating, a growl erupted from her. She could take the deer down in a matter of seconds, or she could alert it to her and enjoy the chase.

Letting another ferocious growl slip from her lips, slightly louder, the animal froze. Slowly, the deer turned its head, and when its black eyes locked on hers, it bolted. She darted between trees, dodging this rock and that fallen branch, all the while keeping a set distance between her and her meal. The fear in the deer sent waves of pheromones that were like a drug to her. As the animal began to lose steam, she sped up, finally allowing herself to run. With a giant leap and mouth agape, she tackled the deer, biting into its warm flesh, blood dripping into her hungry mouth.

The animal only fought back for a moment before it let go and gave into its fate. She devoured each bite. When a snarl came from behind she jumped up, ready to protect her kill. The white wolf stood, eyeing the savory meal behind her. She let out a warning growl, but it made no difference, the white wolf pounced.

It tackled her to the ground, teeth bared and growling. The two beasts rolled about, taking nips at the other whenever they had the chance. But she was faster. And Smaller. And she used that to her advantage. Slipping out from under the white wolf whenever it had thought she was trapped, quickly moving behind it to strike her own attack, only to be over powered moments later.

The battle raged on, covering them both in the blood that had spilled on the ground as well as their own wounds before they had healed. The white wolf no longer white and she could smell the blood drenching her own coat. The sky had begun to lighten, and neither wolf wanted to back down and give into the fatigue until both, still wrapped around one another, succumbed to the fading moon, and passed out. But not before she saw a large black wolf watching from a nearby rock.

~*~

Mackenzie woke with a groan. Her head was pounding, and she felt unusually warm. Warmer than normal for a Werewolf. Slowly opening her eyes, allowing herself time to adjust to the streaming sunlight, she found the reason for the heat. She and Liam were wrapped around each other. Naked and covered in blood.

She knew she should move, but the feeling of being wrapped in his arms and nothing else stirred her desire. She had wanted to be exactly where she was ever since their first date when he held her up against her bedroom door and ravished her with his hand and lips.

She lay still, feeling his chest rise and fall with every warm breath that cascaded over her face. Her arms were pinned in front of her, against the firm planes of his muscles. Her legs, one between his and the other hitched over his hip allowed her to feel the length of him. All she had to do was shift just a bit and they would be perfectly lined up. She felt her own breathes deepen, and the moistness that was collecting between her legs was almost enough to give in to her desires. Her resolve to keep things platonic between them until she chose was weakening.

Liam's eyes fluttered open and his soft features hardened when he saw how the two were wrapped in one another. A fire lit in him like she had never seen and the semi-soft length that had been pressed against her leg hardened. And lengthened.

"Move away now, Mackenzie, or I will kiss you," Liam's voice was rough. She knew he was giving her the chance to keep up with what she had asked of both him and Geoff. While her head told her she should listen to him, her body thought otherwise.

When she didn't respond, he followed through. Crashing his mouth to hers, and pulling her tighter against his body, and he did not disappoint. His fingers kneaded the soft flesh of her back as he deepened their kiss. This was not sweet and special as she had always imagined their first time to be, but primal and urgent. Grinding her hips into his, he let out a groan.

Reaching down, he gripped her thigh and pulled the leg that lay between his to the side, wrapping it around his other hip. He bent down, taking her nipple into his mouth in such a way that made Mackenzie throw her head back and moan in ecstasy. Her hands moved to his head and threaded through his hair, holding him tightly to her breast.

"Does this mean the platonic line has erased? I would love to know for future reference an all. But do carry on fucking him right in front of me." Mackenzie and Liam froze with Geoff's harsh words. With the moment effectively doused in cold water, the two pulled apart to see Geoff sitting on a rock not too far from where they were.

"No. I don't know. I don't know what the hell I want, and that's the damn problem! I got caught up in the moment. I didn't expect to find myself in that situation. I'm sorry you had to see that. But that hurt that I see that you are feeling right now? That is exactly why I wanted that platonic line, as you put it. I didn't want to hurt either of you."

"Great job you did of that." Geoff stood as he threw the backpack Mackenzie had kept all of her things in down to her. She dressed quickly, ignoring the smearing of blood that covered her body. When they got to a lake or stream, she would take care of it. What mattered now was getting herself clothed and away from Liam. As much as it pained her to walk away without looking at him, she had to, or she might not be able to go.

By the time all three had fallen in step with each other, not a single one talking, Mackenzie had thought her headache would have subsided. She hadn't had a single one since her change, not any form of sickness, actually.

"My head is pounding. Do either of you by any strange chance have an aspirin?" When packing her bag after leaving the pack house, she had made sure to grab clothing and her girly products (tampons was such a gross word in her opinion), but she hadn't grabbed any pain pills or medicines. She didn't have any to grab.

"You have a headache?" Geoff asked in alarm. He stopped moving forward and began searching her eyes and feeling around her skull.

"Yeah, is that unusual?" His alarm was scaring her. Could she be a defective wolf? They already knew she was doing things she shouldn't be able to do, so perhaps it wasn't an advantage but a sign of an impending big bad thing bound to happen just because her name was Mackenzie Duncan. It's not like she has ever had the best luck in life. An overbearing mother who never expected she would amount to anything other than a wife so why even try, a father who was in and out of jail on drug and violence charges up until she was eight when he went away for good, growing up barely having the money to put food on the table, let alone wear anything other than thrift store finds that typically didn't fit well anyway, and finally, when she thought her life was about to turn around for good, she gets bitten by a Werewolf while attending Harvard University. Yeah, she had all the luck.

"Highly." The concern for her was etched all over his face. Taking a deep breath, he leaned forward and pressed his lips to her forehead. At first, she thought he was showing her a sign of affection, while trying to maintain the friendship boundary she had set (even though she had broken it into a million pieces just before with Liam,) but when he pulled back, he informed her that she was running hot, even for a Werewolf.

"But why?"

"The only thing I can think of is The Tempering. Remember the analogy you were given? The human body can only take so much change. You are forcing your body, somehow, to progress faster than normal. This has to be because of that. Your human side is rebelling. I've never seen anything like it before."

"Well, there isn't another full moon for a month at least, so maybe my body will have time to adjust before then." The fact that her body was rebelling scared her. In the midst of the issues they all woke to find, the naked and almost fucking thing, none had mentioned the previous night. How early had she turned? Searching her mind, she tried to see if she could remember anything from the night before and was pleased to know that she did. She remembered playing with the white wolf, then her hunt (which sent an involuntary shiver down her spine,) and the fight.

Waking up in Liam's arms and not Geoff's told her that the white wolf was indeed Liam and the black wolf Geoff. She only remembered seeing Geoff in the very beginning before they all ran off in separate directions. She racked her brain and couldn't remember him besides that. It shouldn't surprise her, though, because even her memory of her time with Liam's wolf was spotty.

"How early did I change? I know it was before the moon forced the two of you, but by how much?"

"Just a few seconds. We didn't even have time to react. I wasn't going to say anything just in case the moon did cause your change and not you. I know you have been working on it and didn't want to get your hopes up." At least Geoff was being honest. He could have lied and told her what she wanted to hear instead of the truth.

"I stopped thinking about what makes me remember my time and allowed myself to think like an animal. I thought maybe that's what did it. But I figured I would be giving up the memories that way, but I didn't! I remembered more about last night than usual."

"I remember flashes. The whole concentrating on what you love thing really works.

Mackenzie, your wolf is marble colored, right? Or what do they call it? Brindle?" Liam asked with a hopeful lilt to his voice.

"I have no idea, honestly." And she didn't. She had never put too much thought into what her wolf actually looked like color wise. She had always pictured a snarling mass of fur hiding in dark shadows waiting to attack anything that walked by.

"Yes, Mackenzie is a brindle of light browns and black. Quite stunning, actually." A blush rose to her cheeks at his open appraisal of the darkest part of her. At least, to her it was. Perhaps to a born were, the look of ones wolf could be quite attractive. Turning from him with a small smile, she gave her attention back to Liam.

"If you remember that, then I think you are definitely progressing! That's great. Now we just need to spread the word to any newly bitten. If we could all get control faster, it wouldn't be so scary, and there wouldn't be so many new attacks."

"It does make it easier to handle. I know the idea of two years, twenty-four cycles, without any clue what I was doing, or who I was hurting, terrified me. Knowing I can at least help the process along is really amazing." Liam breathed a sigh of relief, and Geoff watched their exchange carefully.

"It is good news. We should keep moving. The next forty miles are pack territory. They are small and usually harmless, but I would rather not take any more chances. When you regain your strength and the headache has subsided, we will get back to training."

NINE

Mackenzie was sitting on the ground and leaning against a tall tree watching the boys throwing punches at each other over and over. Geoff had decided that Liam had the basics of grappling and wanted to focus more on the typical fighting techniques. Apparently, knowing both was a huge advantage since most packs simply taught their warriors to tackle the enemy as quickly as possible and end the fight just as quickly.

It had been a week since Geoff had let Mackenzie train with him and Liam. Even though her headache only lasted a few days, he was wary of stressing her body any further than it already was. She wasn't sure if she was touched at his concern or irritated for holding her back. Perhaps a bit of both, but either way, she was no longer going to just sit back.

She pushed herself off the ground and strode toward them, determination in her eyes. She would not back down, not even if she had to pick a fight with

Geoff herself. Neither man paid any attention to the fact that she was approaching, both too caught up in their session. It was only when Mackenzie jumped in and caught Liam's fist in her hand, that the men noticed her.

"What the hell? I could have hurt you." Liam was still in his primal mode, the fury raged in his eyes at the same time she could see him battling for control.

"But you didn't because I caught your fist. You didn't hit me because I was faster than you. It's about damn time I get back to training with the both of you." She looked between the two as if she just expected them to argue with her. When they didn't, she smiled triumphantly.

"Fine, but you have to prove you are back to your full strength and speed. Come on, take me down." Geoff's words were laced with the humor he was attempting to hold back. The smirk on his face with his challenge told her that he really didn't think she was capable of doing so. In all honestly, she knew she wasn't. Yet, it wasn't in her nature to back down. From anyone.

Instead of responding to him verbally, she charged. She was fast, as fast as she ever was, and the widening of Geoff's eyes told her he saw it, too. She may not have the experience or the strength that he did, but she was faster than him. She had proved it time and again. Mackenzie knew the chance of taking him down was slim, but perhaps if she could keep him from taking her down it would prove she was ready to start learning again.

She collided with Geoff's legs, but instead of tumbling to the ground, he shifted his weight and threw her to the side. She hit the ground and rolled. Just as she got her feet under her, she saw him lunge. Moving as quickly as she could, she darted out of the way. They continued on like this for almost fifteen minutes, Liam laughing hysterically off to the side at the game of cat and mouse, where both thought they were the cat.

"Enough. Okay, you made your point. I'm done running around already."

"Good, now, show me that throw you used on Liam earlier."

~*~

After hours of training, the three sat around a fire and ate a meal that Liam had caught. They talked and laughed easily as if they were the best of friends without a care in the world. As if they weren't being chased down by their pseudo family, or that the three had some serious sexual tension floating through the air. It was nice, and it showed her what a pack really could be. They may not have a house or money, but they had each other, and they were taking care of each other no matter what else was going on. Perhaps, in spite of what else was going on.

Liam poured water on top of the flames after their meal was complete, sending a plume of smoke into the air. Excusing herself, she left the men to take a walk to not only take care of her full bladder, but for a bit of alone time. She couldn't practice trying to change on will with an audience, and she didn't want to hear any arguing about pushing her body too hard. She managed to overcome the headache just fine. It made sense to her that whatever part of the tempering process that had caused the headache was done, and doing the same wouldn't result in the same after effects. It's not like there was anyone to ask or books to read on the subject.

Mackenzie found a clear spot just a five minute walk from where they were camped out and stripped down to nothing. She knew now to give into her animal instincts, not fight them, when she wanted to change. So she did.

She allowed her senses to take over, her thoughts and feelings to be unbound by human nature. She felt feral. She felt wild. But no matter how much she called on her wolf, she didn't change. The only problem with allowing herself to give into instinct, meant she didn't have control over any emotion, including the irritation and anger she felt at failing yet again.

After three hours of failed attempts, she screamed out in a rage as she ripped a branch from a tree and smashed it against the bark. A masculine scent filled the air that no one other than Geoff had. Turning to see him watching her, with his dark eyes and strong features, arms crossed and eyebrows raised in question, did things to her. Her lust for him untamed, she charged.

Jumping up onto him, she didn't even need him to catch her as her arms and legs locked around him, holding herself up. Nipping his neck and licking a soft and seductive trail up to his ear, she growled, "I need you."

Geoff, taken by surprise growled right back. His hands instinctively circled around her and pulled her tight to him, her breasts pressed tight to him allowing him to feel the firmness of her nipples through his shirt. Mackenzie tried to grind onto him, get him to respond to her.

"Stop. Mac, think. Pull back and get control. You don't want this. Remember who you are, and why you have kept this exact thing from happening. Take a deep breath and think, damn it."

Slowly, Mackenzie's heart rate slowed and the rough material of his jeans no longer felt amazing but scratchy against her nether region. Taking a deep breath, embarrassment flooded her. Dropping her legs, she hopped down, hoping he would release her so she could go and hide until the red that was sure to spring up had a chance to subside. How could she have let herself get so caught up? She hadn't lost that kind of control in so long.

Geoff didn't let go of her, though. He held her to him and looked down at her. She could feel his eyes staring at her, and she couldn't look up at him. When his free hand rubbed her arm, then tipped her chin in his direction with a soft nudge of his fingers, she had no choice but to look at him.

"Hey, don't. This never happened. You lost control, which you hardly ever do. Nothing to be embarrassed about."

"Never happened." Mackenzie knew that he was trying to help her get over what had just happened, but those two words stung. After his constant rejection of her back at the house, and him pushing her away in front of everyone until he saw that she was becoming invested in someone else, saying 'never happened' was like sending an ice pick through her wolf-hot heart.

"Why don't you put your clothes back on, and tell me what the hell you are doing out here?"

Mackenzie walked away from Geoff. She needed distance, and even though her clothes were only a few feet from him, she scooped them up and went even further. Slipping out of the small clearing, she hid behind a tree to dress. What the hell was wrong with her? He was only doing what she asked of him. He could have easily given in and had his way with her, effectively ruining the whole no touching rule she set forth, especially after the fiasco between her and Liam that Geoff had to see. Maybe he didn't want to touch her that way and just didn't want Liam to touch her either. Maybe he was back to his "wolves don't do this unless they are forever" mating crap.

She dressed, and wiped the stray tear that had fallen from her eye, before stepping back into the clearing where Geoff was still waiting. Neither said anything and just stared at each other.

"I'm waiting." His arms were crossed, and he began to stare at her as if she were a child being scolded.

"Keep acting like that, and you can wait forever, for all I care."

"I have forever, remember? Stop being petulant and tell me."

"Forget it, doesn't matter anyway. Didn't work." Mackenzie thought that she was closing the conversation. She tried to walk passed Geoff to go back to camp, but he stepped to the side, blocking her path.

"Tell me."

"No."

"Damn it, Mac. You are not leaving here until you do."

"Oh, are you my dad all of a sudden? Oh wait, he is still sitting in lock up. Pretty sure that role is covered even if he does suck at it."

"No, not your fucking dad. Just someone who cares about you and about keeping the three of us alive and ready for the next round of "Margret wants us dead." Get over yourself and think about the rest of us. We all need to be on the same damn page."

"I was trying to change, okay? I did it once early, why not now? If I can learn how to do that, then we have a better chance at not dying in the next fight."

"Unless you force too many damn changes at once and your body shuts the fuck down. Do you not remember the headache? What if that was just the beginning?"

"It doesn't even fucking matter, Geoff! I couldn't do it. Could. Not. Do. It. I can't fight, I can't shift. I can't even fucking figure out my own heart and give the two of you an answer! Just let me go to sleep."

Without another word, Geoff moved out of her way. Mackenzie walked back to their camp site and could feel his eyes on her, but yet didn't hear a sound. Perhaps he had thinking of his own to do.

TEN

Things were strained between Mackenzie and Geoff. Liam watched the two closely, but never asked what had happened. The scowl on his face told Mackenzie that he most likely thought something physical. It had, but not in the way he was thinking.

"Okay, are we going to be coming up to civilization any time soon? I really want a hot shower. My hair is disgusting." Mackenzie rarely complained about their circumstances. It was her idea to leave Margret's pack to begin with. But it had been weeks and washing in the cold streams they had come across just wasn't doing it for her anymore.

"Not really sure. The area looks different than the last time I came through here."

"Are we lost?" Liam finally spoke. He had been silent the whole day, and Mackenzie was beginning to worry about him, but didn't want to ask until they could actually have time to talk.

"Not sure. Let's just keep going. Eventually, we have to come out on the other side of the forest."

Mackenzie wasn't so sure. What if they were walking in circles? It wasn't as if they didn't know how or couldn't actually survive in the wilderness. They had been doing it for over a month, but she had so hoped for a hot shower, a soft bed, and maybe even a bagel for breakfast instead of fire-roasted rabbit.

Geoff stopped walking and turned in a circle, taking in everything. With a giant sigh, he pointed to the south east and said, "This way. Gotta be this way."

Not really believing him, but not having any other suggestions, Mac and Liam followed along behind him.

Sounds of children playing filled the silence they had been walking in. A smile fell upon Mackenzie's face. Perhaps Geoff knew where he was going after all. Even if the road wasn't just ahead, surely the people there could tell them which way to go.

"Come on!" Liam shouted and ran ahead. Geoff and Mackenzie tried yelling after him, telling him it might not be a great idea to rush into a group of children in the woods, but it was no use. He was running full speed ahead and all they could do was catch up.

~*~

Ten children were jumping around, throwing a ball back and forth, throughout the trees, and moving toward a path. The first real path that Mackenzie had seen in weeks. A sigh of relief passed through her lips and as if the children had heard the sound, they all stopped.

As each of their heads turned in the trio's direction, she listened. Their heart beats thrummed beneath their chests just as fast as her own. They darted their eyes around, taking in every detail and she could tell they could see them all. Just as she could. They were Werewolf children. If they hadn't turned for the first time were they considered werewolves yet? Mackenzie had no clue.

"Hello, we kind of lost our way to the road. Do you think you guys could point us in the right direction?" Mackenzie asked. A little girl who looked to be about four nodded her head and ran up, taking Mackenzie's hand and pulling her toward the path. She could hear the other children urging Geoff and Liam along. "What's your name?"

"Layana. What's yours?"

"Mackenzie. And that's Geoff and Liam. They're my friends."

"Come on! This way!" Layana pulled her hand away giggling and ran. Playing along, Mackenzie ran after her.

Voices echoed through the woods, growing louder with every step she took following the little girl. They were about to step foot into another pack. She could only hope that they were a friendly crowd.

They exited the trees to a giant clearing with eight miniature houses made out of tree branches and logs, a fire circle in the center of them and about fifty adults enjoying their day milling about.

"Daddy! This lady and her friends want to find the road, can you help?" Layana called out running straight into the legs of a very tall and very muscular man. He turned and sniffed the air, eyes slightly narrowed and took in Mackenzie, Geoff, and Liam.

"Passing through?" he asked.

"Trying to. We've been traveling since before the last moon, can't seem to find the road into town." Geoff's voice was even, watching the group around them closing in.

"We are sorry to bother you, but we heard the kids playing and haven't seen a single person. It's just time for some actual food and a hot shower. We don't mean to disrupt you all."

"No, it's fine. Ben can show you to the road. Have you had anything to eat yet today? We were about to have some lunch if you are interested in sticking around for a little bit."

"We ca..." Geoff started.

"We would love to," Mackenzie finished, glaring at Geoff. She was hungry and these people seemed nice.

"Great! Nadia, can you go tell Pack Master that we have guests, and ask Vince if he could make sure we have three extra servings." Two others ran off in different directions, presumably following orders.

"What has you three wandering the woods? Where is your pack?"

"We are our own pack. We left the others." Gasps filled the area with her explanation. She had a feeling it wasn't a common thing to defect from a pack, but surely others had to have done it at one point or another since the big split from being led by the Royal Wolf.

"Left? What about the Oath? Do you not feel loyalty to your pack, your family?" Someone shouted from the back. Perhaps being honest hadn't been the best course of action, and the look on Geoff's face said more than his words could have. TOLD YOU SO.

"Liam and I never took the oath. We were not with the pack long enough to do so. Neither of us chose to become what we are, and we are just trying to find a way to live happily with the hand we have been dealt. Staying with that pack was not the answer."

"But who is your leader? Which of you is of royal decent?"

"And what of you, the other, had you taken the oath?"

"They are no pack! They are rogue!"

The comments were coming from every direction, and Mackenzie didn't know which way to turn or who to answer first. What would it matter if anyone was of royal decent? She thought that Margret was the one that mattered to.

"ENOUGH!" A deep voice bellowed from behind the group. It sounded familiar to Mackenzie and sent a shiver up her spine. "These are our guests and we will not question them like criminals. We know nothing of what they have dealt with."

Everyone's questions around her silenced. With heads bowed slightly, they gave a slight murmur of agreement. Slowly turning around to see who owned the voice, her body tensed. It had been a while, but she would never forget his face. His lies.

A growl erupted from her chest, angry and feral. With her eyes locked on him, she pounced.

~*~

A flurry of activity sprang at the exact moment that Mackenzie did. She could hear them all, and feel the tremble of violence in the air, but her eyes were locked squarely on the man in front of her.

With just a few feet between her and the tall man, with dark brown hair and an all too familiar nose, mouth, and chin, she was caught around the middle. With a thud, she was thrown to the ground, all the air escaping her. Gasping for breath, she found herself underneath Ben. His teeth were bared, and he held her to the ground with his hand to her throat.

Clawing at his arm, she thrashed trying to get away. Growls came from all directions, but she couldn't tear her eyes away from her target. He, too, must have felt the same because his eyes were locked on hers.

"STOP! EVERYONE, BACK DOWN!" he bellowed.

"But Sir! She attacked! They attacked!" someone from behind called out.

"She is my daughter."

The pack went silent. The hand at her throat was gone in an instant, and as the breath returned to her, she sobbed.

Within seconds, she was surrounded by arms. Liam on one side of her, Geoff on the other. They held her, rocked her, and just let her get it out. She never looked up at them, but she could only hope they were glaring at her father in the way that she wished she could do in that moment.

ELEVEN

"Leave us. I must talk with my daughter." The pack made themselves scarce. Some headed into the trees and others into their houses, but all that remained were looking between her and her friends and their pack master. "I said leave. I do not believe she will try to attack again."

Slowly, what Mackenzie assumed was his second and third in command, left them by the fire pit in the center of their little Werewolf community. Mackenzie wiped her tears from her face and gave Liam and Geoff's arm a squeeze before standing up.

She wished she could be eye-to-eye with her father, but even with her two-inch growth after becoming a Werewolf, she was still almost a foot shorter than he was. She remembered looking up to him as a child and wondering if he was as tall as a tree. She begged him to take her outside and stand next to one so she could compare. When he did, she climbed up his body with his help, and sat on top of his shoulders, marking the tree. He wasn't quite as tall, but she was convinced that he would keep growing.

She shook her head from the memory, one of the few good ones she had of him, and stared, waiting for an explanation. She deserved one. Pack Master? How could that be? Had he gotten out of jail only to be turned? But then why hadn't he returned? But then again, she ran from her human life, too.

What about the letters? She would send them to the prison. He would write back sometimes, and never once was his response pleasant. How had he managed to gain a pack so quickly?

"You have questions." His statement was so plain, no feeling in them. Of course she did.

"You're observant." Mackenzie's voice dripped with the hurt and the anger that had been brewing beneath the surface for so many years.

"Ask. I will answer."

"How about you start with the fucking fact that you are a god damn Werewolf!" She screamed. Her voice cracked with the force. Liam reached out for her hand, but she jerked away. She didn't want his calming touch. She wanted to be angry. She deserved to be angry.

"I was born a Were. My Father was the pack master before me, and his father before him. It is my bloodline. Our bloodline. Although I never thought I would see the day you stood before me with the moon's force cycling through your veins."

"But I was bitten! I wasn't born. Mom isn't a Werewolf."

"No, she isn't. I met your mother one day when I decided to travel. I took a vacation from pack life. When you live with the same people for so long, there comes a time when you want to escape for brief periods. When I met her, I fell for her. She was human, and my pack wouldn't understand. So I stayed away. Then she got pregnant with you. I was to be a father to a human child. I knew the biology of Were reproduction, but I was actually happy. I wouldn't have to see my child go through the pain of their first cycle, and I wouldn't have to see them feel like an outsider among other children in school. They would grow up, be happy, get married, have babies, and die a normal human life.

"At times, there is nothing you want more than a 'normal' life. Bitten or born, we know how easy humans have it. I wanted that for you. When the moon cycles started affecting me more and more, I lost control. I was arrested over and over. But I don't have to tell you that. You were there. I saw the hurt in your eyes with every court date and cop showing up at our door."

"And the drugs?" she asked. She wasn't sure what she thought, but she wanted all the information. Mackenzie had started pacing in front of the fire. When she looked up, she could see the red glow that framed Liam, watching her carefully with a look of pure concern. Geoff was glaring at her father with what could only be described as hatred. She understood how he felt.

"There were never any drugs. It was the best excuse to explain the strength that I had."

"Did Mom know?"

"That I was a Werewolf? Not at first, but after a while of disappearing once a month without any real explanation, she followed me. She tried to understand. She loved me. She loved you and our family. But in the end, it was too much for her. When she saw the amount of violence I was capable of, she sent me away. Told me never to come back and to not contact either of you again. I shouldn't have listened to her, but the idea of hurting you by accident was devastating. As a born, I have more control over my actions and strength then a bitten, and as a pack leader, I have more than most, but there are always accidents.

"Do you remember that day when you were about four and wanted to measure me against the tree?"

"Yeah, I do. What about it?" She was still angry, but in a much more subdued way. She was out of energy to scream, and she was tired. With a heavy heart, she sat and watched the man that gave her life, that held her as a small child, and that had abandoned her.

"You almost fell from my shoulders. I reached up to catch you and left bruises on your arms for days. The preschool sent a child services worker to the house to investigate. I told them what happened, and they agreed it was an accident that happened in your best interest. That was just one time. When your mother told me to leave, that she couldn't handle my secret or my outbursts any more, I listened. I did go to jail, but I was out within days. I wrote you letters and tried to call, but your mother intervened. Said a clean break was what you all needed."

"I never got any letters unless I sent one to the prison first. Did you start writing back those nasty letters to keep me from wanting a connection with you? It would have been better to just be ignored."

"I told you, I left the prison within days. I received no letters from you. It broke my heart, but after everything I put you through, I thought you deserved a better life. I wrote to you on your birthday every year and sent gifts every Christmas. Did you not receive any of those?" His calm facade faltered. A fire lit in his own eyes and for the first time, she felt sympathy for her father. He hadn't abandoned them the way she had thought. He had left, yes, but it was to protect her. How could she be mad at that when she had done the same thing?

"No. I never got a present from you."

He took a deep breath, pacing back and forth, wringing his hands, and cracking his knuckles. She remembered this look. He did this when Mackenzie was little, when she had broken the vase full of flowers he had bought for her mother before she had seen them. She knew he was attempting to calm himself down.

"Can I ask a question now?" His voice was low and trembling. He looked up and gave her a sad smile. Mackenzie nodded, urging him to ask. "How was it after I left?"

"At first, it was sad. We moved so the kids wouldn't tease me, and so Mom could find a job. We moved a lot. We didn't have a lot of money. I did really well in school, even though I was held back the year you left. I got a scholarship to Harvard."

Mackenzie watched her father's eyes light up with pride. It was the look she had hoped to see from her parents when she got her acceptance letter but never did. Her mother was convinced she wasn't ready to be so far away on her own in a school that expected so much of their students, and her father's letter was heartbreaking, to say the least. Or, the letter she received from someone she thought was her father.

"I am so proud of you. You are so grown up. So beautiful."

"How did you know it was me? I was eight the last time you saw me."

"A father knows his daughter. I am so sorry, Mackenzie. So sorry. I wish I had been there for you. Been there when you turned. Who bit you? When?"

"How about I start at the beginning?"

The four werewolves sat around the fire as Mackenzie told her story. She started with the horrible walk home from the football game where she kneed an asshole in the balls for picking a fight. She told him how the wolf attacked her, and how she bashed its head in with a rock before crawling away as her body healed itself. She told him how for weeks she had no idea what was going on with her and how she was terrified of the changes in her strength and appearance and miraculous healing and how she ran away from everything after she turned the first time. She told him how Margret had found her and took her in, leaving out the bloody and horrible morning where she buried her first human kill with Geoff, and how she turned Liam. When she told him of the plan she had uncovered, she could see how livid her father was. She didn't blame him. If it were up to Margret, every pack master would be dead, and she would control every Werewolf in the world.

"Your life has been anything but easy in the last few months. I should have been there for you, welcomed you into my pack when you turned. I didn't know, and I should have. I can never make it up to you, but I would love it if you and your friends stayed here, with us."

"We were really looking forward to hitting up a hotel for beds and showers," Geoff said before Mackenzie could answer. He was right they were, but this was her father. Her father was right in front of her after so many years and he wanted her. He wanted her.

"I understand." Her father's voice was so defeated. Mackenzie couldn't help but reach out to him. When their hands touched, she felt that familiar comforting buzz under her skin that she always felt around her own kind, at least when danger wasn't lurking around the corner, but times a million. She pulled back as if she was electrocuted. He reached out for her again and held on. The current passed through him and into her and back. It was nothing she had ever felt before. She could feel her father's love for her. A tear fell from her eye.

"What was that?"

"That was blood recognizing blood. We have so much more to discuss, but I think first food is in order. If your friends wish to go to a hotel in town, I can have Ben take them. I really would like you to stay."

Mackenzie knew that they shouldn't split up. She wasn't afraid for herself. Her father would never hurt her. At least, she didn't believe he ever would. She looked to Geoff and Liam pleadingly. They, too, knew they should stick together, and if they still insisted on the hotel, she would go with them.

"Mackenzie, if you want to stay, I will stay with you," Liam gave her a soft smile. She had talked with him in detail about her father before. He knew exactly what this meant to her. She looked to Geoff who huffed and sighed, then finally nodded his head in agreement.

"Good, it's settled. Let's get some rooms set up for you all. It may not look like it, but these houses do have beds, and we have a camping shower set up about ten minutes outside of our living space."

The boys were led off to two other houses side by side, and Mackenzie's father led her in another direction.

"My house is that one, please, make yourself at home. I must take care of a few things within the pack, and I will be right there." He pointed in the direction of a house that was the exact same as all the others were, only it was at the head of the arrangement of houses, much like the head of a table. He was much humbler about his position than Margret ever was. She was all about the opulence and showing off her superiority among the pack. Her father, from what she had seen so far, just wanted to be one of the pack, only showing his authority when he needed to.

Mackenzie was in a small room in her father's little house. She could tell that other people lived with him, and for a brief moment, she was in shock. But it had been twelve years since he left her mother, so of course he would have moved on. He was a pack master, and that meant he had to have a mate and with mate's came a child. Did she have a sibling yet? A brother or a sister? Or both?

The house had a small living space and two sectioned off sleeping areas. There were beds in both, but one had a much larger bed than the other. She instinctively headed to the area with the smaller bed and climbed in. Food could wait. It had been a long day and an even longer night and she was exhausted.

~*~

"Mackenzie?"

Groaning at the sound of her name being called and waking her from the best sleep she had had in weeks, Mackenzie attempted to burrow deeper under her covers and pull the pillow tight against her head. It was something that Teresa would have done. She missed her old room-mate but knew there was nothing she could do about it. Perhaps their paths would cross again when there wasn't so much tension between her and her old pack. At least she really hoped so.

"What?" she asked without coming out of her hiding spot.

"I thought you might be hungry. I sent a few members into town to get you and your friends some food that wasn't wild game. Thought maybe you would rather some greasy breakfast sandwiches from this little diner we frequent."

Mackenzie sniffed the air, and sure enough, she smelled bacon. Flinging the covers off her, she was up and in front of her father in seconds. He was beaming at her, and she hopped from foot to foot waiting for him to hand it over. He laughed at her, and when she saw his hands were empty, she pouted. She felt like a child, but the promise of bacon to only be denied was just not nice.

"Don't do that. You know I could never say no to that face. It's on the table. Go on. I will get Geoff and Liam, and send them in. I'm sure you three have some things to talk about."

Mackenzie watched him walk out the door, and instantly, she felt like the eight-year-old child watching her father walk out of the courtroom and into custody. She stood and ran to the door to watch him. How was it possible that she had never known who he really was? For the first time in a long time, she was absolutely furious with her mother. She wasn't just upset or disappointed in her, she was livid. How dare she keep her from her father, while parading men in and out of her life trying to find a replacement? How dare she make her believe that he was a no good piece of shit who didn't care about her? She had figured it out. Her mother must have intercepted the letters and written her own responses. She knew that the world of werewolves was scary, but when Mackenzie grew up she had a right to know who she was, and who her father was.

When she saw that he knocked on one door, and Liam's blond mop of hair came into view, she returned to the table to start eating. There were a pile of bacon and egg sandwiches on the table, and she knew if she didn't start then, the boys would come in and devour them without her getting her fill, too.

She was two sandwiches in when the boys walked through the door. They both sat down at the small table and dug in. No one actually spoke until just crumbs remained on the table between them.

"Do you believe him?" Geoff asked, looking directly at Mackenzie.

"Of course I do. Why would he lie about that?" Mackenzie was instantly on the defensive. She knew it wasn't reasonable. He may be her father, but she didn't really know him. Geoff had been there for her from the beginning and left with her when she couldn't take living with Margret a second longer.

"Calm down, it's just a question. I don't know why he would lie. I don't know him, but neither do you. It's obvious that he is your father—just looking at the two of you next to each other is enough proof of that. But if he really did want you all this time, why didn't he go looking for you when you turned eighteen? Your mother had no say at that point. He didn't."

"Dude, chill out. Let her figure this out on her own. We don't know what she is going through."

"I was an orphan. I know what it's like to not have a parent, and I tell you what, if I ran into one who all of a sudden 'loved' me to death and wanted me around, I would be suspicious. Especially after learning that I was in another pack. What if he just wants Intel?"

"He hasn't asked anything about Margret's pack." Mackenzie wouldn't look at Geoff. Her arms were crossed, and she stared out the window by the front door, pleading with her eyes to stay dry.

"Because you already told him she was planning on taking her royal position back. He wants to keep you around to ask more questions later. I'm telling you, he will come and ask more."

"Who wouldn't want more information after finding out an attack is coming? We warned the other pack, why not my father's? I think every pack has a right to know." Her voice was quivering and she knew it. She was glad that neither man mentioned it.

She felt Liam's hand rest on her thigh under the table, and she chanced a glance in his direction. He wasn't looking at her but at Geoff with irritation.

"Seriously, let's drop it for now, okay? He is a pack master, so maybe he can help us get the word out faster or help us find a place to set up on our own."

"Mac, I won't be joining his pack. I agreed to leave to start out on our own, not fall into another pack. I know he is your father, but I draw the line with devoting myself to another pack leader. I left Margret for you, a woman who has been like my mother for a very long time. Don't ask me to disrespect her even more by joining another."

"I wouldn't ask you to. I don't even know if I want to be in a pack after the last one, but I do want to spend some time getting to know him. If you want to go to town for a few days, I get it. But I'm not going anywhere just yet."

"Whatever you decide, I'm with you, Mackenzie," Liam said. She gave him a small smile and then the three just looked around the table. It was the first real test of their loyalty to one another. Mackenzie knew she was the one throwing a wrench in the plans, whatever plans those may be, but it was her father. How could she walk away without finding out everything she could?

A knock at the door startled them all. Mackenzie stood and just as she was about to grab the doorknob, it opened. She took a step back and watched as a tall and absolutely beautiful woman walked through. Her dark hair flowed over her shoulders in perfect ringlets and her skin was a decadent caramel color. Dark eyes finished off the look that could only be described as exotic.

"I didn't mean to startle you, but your father sent me for you. He would like more of a chance to talk."

"Yeah, we were just finishing up in here. I'm sorry. I don't think we met last night in all of the crazy that happened."

"We did not. I was at the house in town with the children that are in school. They stay there during the school year. My name is Nadia. It is so nice to finally meet you. Darren has always spoken so fondly of you."

"Darren?" Geoff asked from the table, standing abruptly.

"Yeah, that's my father's name. What did you think his name was, Dad the Pack Leader?" Mackenzie asked with sarcasm. A look of recognition fell over Geoff, but he quickly calmed his features. Mackenzie took note and planned to ask him about it the next time they were alone.

"Of course not. If you need us, we will be wandering around."

"This way Mackenzie," Nadia said and motioned to follow with a nod of her head.

~*~

Nadia lead Mackenzie into the forest back the way she had come in with the children. The warming weather had allowed the trees and plants to flourish in the way that only happened in the spring. It was becoming beautiful instead of the desolate whites and greys she had been living with for months. It was a welcome sight.

They found her father sitting on a fallen log by the edge of a small pond. He was staring out over the water and looked completely relaxed. She knew he heard their approach, so she didn't say anything. She just went and sat down next to him. Nadia stayed a few feet behind and watched them.

Mackenzie looked back at her in question, but she just smiled and shook her head. She was giving them some space. Mackenzie just wasn't sure why she wasn't leaving them alone. Surely they didn't believe she would attack him again, and even if she had, there would be no way she would ever actually be able to harm him.

She heard her father sigh before he tore his eyes from the water to look at her. Staring into his face she was able to see exactly how much they looked alike. She used to have his eyes, too, but that changed when she was bitten. Her eyes were permanently the yellowish-green, her deep brown forever lost. Another bonus for being born a Were. They only had the freaky eyes when they actually turned into a wolf.

"Can I hug you? It has been—"

She didn't let him finish his sentence. She launched herself into his arms and held on tight. When she felt his arms wrap around her, enveloping her in his warmth, she lost all composure. She allowed her tears to flow free. She let all the anger and pain and heart break flow out of her with each tear drop.

Only when she felt her own shoulder begin to dampen, did she realize that he too was crying. He began to mumble words of apology over and over. It was when she heard the words 'I love you' that she pulled back and looked at him. She had memories of him saying that from before he left, but she never allowed herself to think of them. Too many bad memories happened after and she thought her mind was playing tricks on her, wanting her to believe something that wasn't true.

"What did you say?" she asked through sniffles, wiping the tears from her eyes.

"I said, I love you. I always have and missing out on your life was a mistake I will never make up for in the rest of our days. I should never have let your mother talk me into leaving you."

"I love you, too. I am still trying to figure this all out in my head. What was real and what wasn't. I have spent so many years with just these letters that I thought were from you, these horrible mean words. I just need time. If I hadn't been bitten, I never would have found you. Imagine that, something good actually coming out of the worst thing to happen to me in my entire life."

"Is it horrible that I am glad it happened only because you found me? That I can explain everything to you, everything you ever wanted to know and not hold anything back? You are my daughter, my eldest daughter, which gives you rank in my pack."

"I don't want to be part of your pack, Dad. I just left a pack. It was all nice and wonderful on the surface, but the minute you started to scratch the surface, it was vile and just wrong in so many ways. Plus, I'm bitten. We can't hold rank within a pack."

"Not that pack, but a biological child being bitten is a rare occurrence. You have more Were in you than other bittens. Tell me, how long have you been cycling?"

"Six months. The longest six months of my life."

"And you have control of your emotions?"

"Well, most of the time." She flushed thinking of her attacking Geoff insistent on having him.

"I see. Those two traveling with you? Which of them is your mate?" he asked with a smile.

"Neither. It's a long story that I would really rather not get into right now."

"I understand. Speaking of matters of the heart, Mackenzie, there is much to tell you about my life now. I want you to know everything." Her father turned and looked at Nadia, who Mackenzie had forgotten was even there she was so quiet, and motioned for her to join them. As soon as Nadia sat down beside her father, she knew what he was going to tell her.

"Nadia is your mate?"

"Yes, she is. We met and mated eight years ago. She is the third woman to ever capture my heart." He looked into Nadia's eyes and squeezed her hand, before turning back to Mackenzie.

"Third?"

"Of course. Your mother was the first, and you, beautiful daughter, the second."

"Oh. Right. So, step-mother?" Mackenzie looked to Nadia for the answer. This was brand new territory for everyone involved and she was looking for her reaction.

"Only if you want to consider me that. Our pack has a very community way of raising children, but you are long passed that stage. I would like to be your friend, though."

"Okay. What about siblings? Do I actually have a brother or a sister?"

"Lyla. She is seven and is staying up at the house in town. The children attend school as soon as they are old enough and up until they begin to show signs of the impending change in puberty. Then, we switch them to the homeschooling program. If we are going to live for hundreds of years, being educated in the way the world works is important."

That made perfect sense to Mackenzie, and she loved that school was important to them. It meant that her and her father had something in common, a love of knowledge.

"I can't wait to meet her. What's she like?"

Her father and Nadia went on to tell her all about her sister. She sounded like a normal seven year old girl who just happened to have werewolves for parents. She was active, had friends, and was really great at reading. She apparently also knew she had an older sister, but that they didn't know where she was. It warmed Mackenzie's heart to know that her father did care and always had. He had spoken of her to his new family and never tried to hide her existence, even though she was born human.

When Mackenzie's stomach growled loudly, they realized just how long they had been gone. Walking back together, Mackenzie smiled. She knew they still had a lot to talk about, but she was okay with that.

TWELVE

Geoff and Liam were sitting with a few of the pack members when they returned from the little pond. Both men stood up as soon as she came into view, and she could see the look of worry on their faces. She smiled at them, hoping to let them know she was fine and they could relax.

Liam smiled back at her, but Geoff's eyes darted to her father and Nadia's clasped hands. When he looked back to her, he had a questioning look on his face, but she kept her smile. There was nothing to be worried or concerned about, and he needed to trust her.

"Family, gather around the meeting place, please. I believe it is time for a long overdue introduction. Perhaps one without all the fighting?" her father called out.

There were a few chuckles among the group, but everyone began walking to the center circle of the house and sitting around the hollowed out ground that had ash and burnt pieces of wood in the bottom. Liam and Geoff made their way over to her side. The three of them positioned themselves toward the back of the group. This wasn't their pack, and while Mackenzie knew she was to be introduced as his daughter, she wasn't in her pack. The direct circle should be pack members only, and when she was introduced, and no sooner, would she move forward.

"Everything go okay?" Liam whispered so low his breath and the soft hum of his words tickled her ear. Mackenzie grasped his hand and squeezed, nodding. It had gone well. She was actually on her way to happiness, and she knew it was because of the three men that were now part of her life. Maybe being turned was not just the worst thing to happen to her, but somehow also the best. Maybe this was exactly the life she was meant to have. Her father was a pack leader, after all.

"You are all my family. You are all my pack. You have stood by my side, even when I strayed into the human world and welcomed me back with open arms. When my mother passed, you all turned to me and consoled me for my loss at the same time as declaring your loyalty to me as your new leader. Today, I hope you can all welcome my daughter into our family, as well. Even if she doesn't choose to stay with us, she should always be welcome should she return. My blood flows through her veins, our lineage flows through her. Mackenzie, daughter, please, come stand by my side." Her father spoke to his pack in much the way that Margret did. Although his words filled with emotion, were real. She knew in her heart that he was genuine.

Mackenzie slowly moved between the pack to the front. Her father's open arms welcomed her in a hug before turning her to face the pack. Mackenzie smiled at the group of people watching her.

"Elder One, what say you? Born of a pack master's blood into a human body but bitten at such an early age and advancing so quickly. Does she earn the respect of the title of our bloodline?" Her father's eyes searched out an elderly man in the back of the room. He was the eldest looking Werewolf Mackenzie had ever seen.

"What does that mean?" she asked her father, quickly looking back up to him.

"Listen," he whispered, hugging her with one arm and watching the Elder One.

The Elder One stood. His hair had turned grey, and his skin actually held wrinkles. He didn't stand as tall as the others, and his bulk definitely had withered over the years. For a Werewolf, he would be considered a senior citizen, but in human terms, this man could easily still be healthy enough to run around chasing his grandchildren.

"As far back as Gwendolyn, I have never heard of such a case. The question we must ask ourselves is: was her royal blood being awoken a coincidence or an attack against our line? I put it to the pack to vote on if we allow a mix blood, not just human and Were, but human and our royal line with another Were bloodline, to be allowed to lead should her father fall before Lyla is of age. I speak nothing against the girl, but I feel more questions should be asked and answered before that should happen."

The Elder One sat back down, and the silence that had fallen upon the pack when he spoke was quickly filled with a low murmur of agreements, disagreements, and over all confusion. Mackenzie didn't know what was happening and quickly turned to Geoff, desperately hoping he would be able to clarify everything that had been said. When he wouldn't meet her eye, she knew something was wrong.

"Dad? What the hell is he talking about?" she whispered harshly.

"Which part?"

"All of it! Who is Gwendolyn and what royal blood? What does he mean as an attack? Could Margret have known I was your daughter?"

"Did she not give you any history on our ways? On our history?" Her father's irritation seeped through his tone. She was taken aback and went to leave his side. If he wouldn't answer her, she would just have to make Geoff. "Mackenzie, wait. You, Liam, and Geoff should all know our history. You should know who you are. Go and get them. Meet me back at the house. I must discuss this with my pack."

"You know I never agreed to any of this anyway, right? The three of us are plenty happy being together," she reminded him. He just nodded with a sad smile.

"I know, baby girl. I know. I still want to prepare the pack on the off chance that you do choose to return to us, as one of us. That's all."

Mackenzie nodded her understanding and marched off to Liam and Geoff. She would make him talk. He wouldn't have a choice.

"What the hell was that? Why is he even asking them about that? I thought you said you weren't joining his pack? We left a pack to go with you, Mackenzie," Geoff started before she even got next to him. Thankfully, her father's pack was a bit busy and not paying attention.

"Can we please go inside to talk? And he knows that. Just go. We can talk in there, and when I say we will talk, I mean you will talk." Mackenzie glared at Geoff. She hadn't felt the need to look at him in such a way in a long time.

~*~

The noise from outside of the pack discussing Mackenzie's future subsided as Liam shut the door behind him. Standing in the living room of her father's house staring down Geoff, Mackenzie waited for answers. She didn't speak. She didn't think she needed to speak. Geoff should know exactly what she wanted to know. How could he not after that announcement from the Elder One?

"I don't know if she knew who your father is. After everything you told me about him, I'm surprised you even care." Geoff was pacing. He couldn't stand still or look her in the eye. Mackenzie got a horrible feeling in her stomach, and for the first time since she decided to join Margret's pack, she wasn't sure she trusted what Geoff was telling her.

"So it's just a coincidence that Mackenzie is of royal blood, whatever the hell that means. What does that mean?" Liam looked between her and Geoff.

Sometimes it was hard to remember that this whole thing wasn't about her. She really needed to work on that. Liam was just as out of the Werewolf loop as she was. He wanted answers just as much as she did.

Mackenzie moved and placed herself next to Liam. Geoff needed to talk and fast, or she was going to get angry.

"Fine, than start with the Royal bloodline. I thought that was all gone," Mackenzie spoke with conviction. She wanted him to know she was serious and his deep penetrating eyes and flexing muscles were not going to distract her this time.

"I told you about the Royal Were. I told you about Rosalinda and her other, and how Gwendolyn's siblings decided against continuing the monarchy and leaving Werewolves up to their own packs and rules. I never lied to you. I don't know why you are questioning me. When have I ever lied to you?" Geoff had stepped forward as he spoke. He locked eyes with Mackenzie and spoke softly. When he stood before her, he stroked her cheek, as if she were the only one in the room.

Liam cleared his throat, and Geoff removed his hand, ending the caress that had Mackenzie mesmerized. Damn him.

"So what does the royal bloodline have to do with anything if it was ended?" she managed to ask after a moment of self-composure.

"Just because people were allowed to follow their own packs, doesn't mean that anyone decided to leave the pack they were in. Most Weres were happy within their own family. And for the most part, the only ones to go off on their own were the children of the bloodline. You can trace almost all pack leaders, or pack masters as some like to be called, back to royal blood. Some packs have credos that state only a Were of the royal line may take over their pack. Maybe more than just some if what the Elder One said got so many of them in a stir."

"So let me get this straight. Margret is the daughter of the old queen of the Weres. Mackenzie is the daughter of some kind of royal Were, as well, but from one of Margret's aunts?" Liam looked about as confused by the whole thing as Mackenzie felt.

She blew out a hard breath, sending the hair in her face flying off to the side before reaching up and tucking it behind her ear. Mackenzie looked back and forth between the guys before plopping herself down on the couch. There was no reason they all had to stand and pace for this conversation. Maybe sitting down would cool everyone off.

"That's what it sounds like. I don't know which one. That is a question for her father. If he answers her."

"What the hell is that supposed to mean?" Mackenzie stood again. Screw the calming down. Geoff didn't have any reason to be wary of her father. He welcomed them, fed them, and gave them a place to sleep. He hadn't done anything to make them suspicious.

"It means that he left you. He built this whole world where HE is the pack leader after leaving it. He walked away from the Were world. Now that you are one of us, he suddenly wants to be all father-like? He knows you come from Margret's pack… that we all do. What if he just wants Intel? You don't know this man at all."

"Fuck you. He is my father. And even if he does want information on Margret, can you really fucking blame him when she plans on taking over the fucking Werewolf world by *killing* the other pack leaders? We have been over this and over this. If you want to go, then go. I am staying, for a little while at least. If I get myself into trouble by trusting the wrong people, then so be it. Won't be the first time."

"Then fucking *trust me*. I am not Margret. I am here with you. Trust that I didn't know. Trust that I care what fucking happens to you. Trust that I honestly feel like something fishy is going on here." Geoff turned his attention away from Mackenzie and focused on Liam. "Seriously, you and I may not agree on a lot of things, but keeping her safe is one thing we do agree on. Can you at least admit that? Would I put her in harm's way intentionally?"

"No, you wouldn't. Mac, I may question his loyalty to me and to what we are trying to do, but never to you. He wouldn't get you hurt on purpose."

"I know. And I wouldn't get either of you hurt, and I hope you know that. Staying here, with my father, is what I think will keep us safe."

The door swung open and Darren stepped through. All three heads turned in his direction, waiting for him to speak. "I will keep you safe."

"Dad, he didn't—"

"Mackenzie, don't worry about it. I am glad you have someone, two *someones'* for now at least, looking out for you, wanting to keep you safe, and only trusting in themselves to do it. They are protective of you. That is a good thing."

Both Liam and Geoff mumbled thanks to Darren, still apparently embarrassed at being caught speaking ill of him. When he waved them off, they loosened up and moved to the couch, taking a seat on either end. Mackenzie, having no other option, sat between them. When all three were settled, their attention returned to Darren.

"So, this whole royal blood thing? Does that make me some kind of princess?" Mackenzie asked with a slight humor to her voice. She was trying to lighten the mood with a joke. Liam and her father laughed. Geoff scowled. Two out of three, not bad.

"I guess you could say that. My Great Great Grandmother was named Merideth. She was sisters with Rosalinda, the Were Queen. Their mother was the first Werewolf. There are many tales of how Gwendolyn came to be, some speak of magic, others of beastiality, but no one really knows. She never told her children how she came upon her gift, only that it was their duty to fill the world with others like them, like us, and to teach them how to live without the persecution of the humans. When Rosalinda was killed, her only daughter was just a child. So her sisters decided to no longer keep up the monarchy. They felt that the packs had learned how to live and didn't need any further interference. Interference is what had gotten their mother and their sister killed."

Darren was pacing the room but speaking so calmly it was as if he were telling a bedtime fairy tale.

Hell, to most people in the world, that is exactly what he was doing, but to Mackenzie, Liam, and Geoff, he was giving a history lesson.

"Many of the packs still wanted someone to look to as rightful leader. That just always happened to be the daughters, and sometimes sons, of the royal line. As far as I know, most packs can be traced back to one of the three sisters, Margret, Merideth, and Ingred. Some Weres went rogue and started their own packs, but those who still follow the basic laws and customs of our kind are all founded through the royal line."

"Laws and customs?" Mackenzie was enthralled. She wondered how much she was about to hear had made its way into one of her college mythology text books. It felt like so long ago that she was sitting in one of the small classrooms at Harvard.

"Yes, things like keeping our existence a secret, mating laws, sires and the like." Mackenzie knew a bit about all of those, but she had hoped he would go into more detail. She especially wanted to know about the mating laws. "We will sit down soon, and I will answer every question you have. But for now, we need to talk about what just happened out there."

Mackenzie was a little disappointed, but her desire to find out more about the mating she might chose with either Liam or Geoff could wait. Her love life took a back seat to the lives of all the pack leaders in the world.

"What was the consensus? And what did the Elder One mean when he said Mackenzie's royal bloodline was awoken?" Geoff asked directly. If there was one thing Geoff did not do, it was beat around the bush.

"It means that when she was born she had royal blood in her. It was only half and it wasn't dominant because as we know, only the females born Were can give birth to a Were child. Royal blood is stronger than others. Were's with a direct line to Gwendolynn possess stronger traits. They run faster, are stronger, have a better sense of smell, are over all more powerful in every aspect. The fact that Mackenzie already had royal blood, then was turned, gave her body a boost. The foreign wolf's saliva that entered her body recognized her genetics and made her transition that much easier, and is making her adjustment that much faster. I have never seen a tempering end so quickly."

"Wait, if there was only one wolf to start, Gwendolyn, then why aren't all wolves of Royal Blood?" Liam asked. It was a good question, but Mackenzie was more concerned with the fact her father thought she had finished tempering.

"What do you mean my tempering has ended? I still have no control over the wolf, and I only remember bits and pieces."

"Liam, much like with humans, over time bloodlines thin out. The exceptions are direct descendants. When Weres of the past mated with humans it brought in new blood. When those children mated, it mixed bloodlines. The further you go, the thinner the original blood is. So yes, everyone has SOME royal blood, just as all humans have traces of a common ancestor. Mackenzie, you said yourself that you changed before the moon forced you last time. That is control. It may be very minute, but it is more than any other bitten in the history of time. With work, we can get you up to speed. You are my daughter, and I have faith in your abilities."

His complete and total trust in her and her potential sent a smile to her face. Perhaps she could be good at this. At being a Werewolf. If she could learn to control every bit of herself, then she could be a great help to the other packs out there in the dark about Margret. She could protect herself. She could help keep Geoff and Liam safe instead of being the one to be kept safe.

"I would like to work with you, as well. I know that I am far from her level, but anything I can do to increase my chances of protecting myself, and her, I want to do," Liam said. Geoff watched the interaction with curiosity, but said nothing.

"I would be thrilled to work with all of you. Geoff, you are more than welcome to come to our trainings. I know you are a skilled fighter and wolf, and we would be lucky to have you there."

"I'm not sure what I could add. I don't know your style."

"I am sure you know all the styles. At least how to fight against them. Margret is a diligent leader, I am sure. She has been around for many, many years. She is the one of the only original grandchildren to still be leading a pack. And that pack wasn't handed down to her. She built her pack when she was old enough to leave her aunt's pack after her own tempering. Perhaps you could point out some weaknesses we can work on."

"Perhaps." The way the Geoff responded with such a clipped answer spoke volumes. He obviously was still on high alert when it came to helping out any other pack, and Mackenzie wasn't so sure that was a good thing. That was what she was trying to do after all, help others know that danger wasn't too far off.

"So what did the pack decide about me? Not that I'm decided about me, but I would like to know if I'm walking into a group that thinks I'm a spy or something."

"There were a few who were wary. They had heard murmurs about Margret's pack expanding, but not why. Then you show up and tell us what's going on. If you were anyone other than my daughter, I would send you packing faster than a speeding bullet. But you *are* my daughter, and I trust you. And my pack trusts me. You are welcome here as are Liam and Geoff. When the time comes, if it ever does, the pack will vote on if you are to be leader should you chose, and if Lyla is not of age to do so. They could not put you above her. While you are my eldest, she is pure Were, and that is the way of our pack. You would be the first ever bitten to hold the title of Pack Leader."

"And that's because I'm more than just a bitten, right? What exactly am I?"

"We don't have a name for it. Perhaps you will be the only one, perhaps more will surface if Margret did, indeed, plan your change."

Liam's leg bounced on the couch beside her, and Geoff's hands were clenching and unclenching. Both men were on edge, and she didn't blame them. They just took in a lot of information in a small time frame. She needed to talk to them. Alone.

"Daddy? Can I please have some time with these guys to sort through everything?"

"Of course." Darren nodded his head with a small smile and left the house.

Within a second, Geoff was off the couch and pacing the room. His hands would find their way to his hair and run through the dark locks before gripping tightly and releasing just to pace and do it again.

Liam sat still, chewing his bottom lip and staring into nothing, and Mackenzie sat there, looking between the two, unsure of what to say. Fortunately for her, she didn't have to say anything.

Geoff turned abruptly to face them with a look of pure seriousness. "Give me one good reason *besides* the fact that he is your father. One good reason to trust him."

"Are we really back on this?" Mackenzie asked with a scowl.

"What kind of a father leaves his child? What kind of a future leader walks away from his pack to follow a human skirt? He abandoned his family. *Both* of them. At least Margret never did that. She may be a lot of things, but she would never turn family away."

"Wow. Just wow." Mackenzie didn't know what to say to him after that. She knew that Margret had been Geoff's mother figure for over two hundred years, so of course he would be protective of her. But he had left her. He left Margret when he realized she was doing wrong, when he realized she wasn't the woman he thought he knew. Didn't he?

Mackenzie stood up and walked out of the cabin, leaving both Geoff and Liam in her wake.

THIRTEEN

The air left Mackenzie's body in a rush as she landed on the hard ground. Liam had just thrown her using some technique her father said was designed for a person of his stature. He was right. It didn't take Liam any time to perfect the move and have her sailing through the air like a paper airplane, yet landing as hard as a Boeing 357 without landing gear.

"GOOD! Again!" Darren yelled to Liam. Mackenzie brought herself to her knees, breathing slowly. She was tired of being the test dummy, but she just kept reminding herself that her turn would come soon.

"Mac, you okay down there? Do I need to get you a stretcher?" Liam joked. Mackenzie sent him a look that could kill before returning to her feet. The smile fell from Liam's lips and his attention returned to her father. "Maybe we should move onto something else?"

"Good idea," she ground out. When she heard her father chuckle, she turned her attention to him. "How about we try something where I don't fall on my ass?"

"Alright. I want to teach you how to out maneuver your opponent and end a fight if you both manage to fall to the ground and are grappling with one another."

"I don't learn throws?" she asked.

"Not now, you don't. While you're strong, a suitable throw is still hard to do. Your strength needs building before you attempt a throw on a male Were, and I have a feeling that is exactly who you will be fighting. Margret won't be sending out many women into battle. She needs them to grow that pack. This neck hold will work on a woman or a man. If done right, it will completely dislocate their neck. Our bodies heal fast, but a dislocated neck takes longer. If you have to, apply a bit more force, or turn into the wolf, and end them by beheading before they are able to move."

The thought of ripping someone's head off made Mackenzie's stomach turn. She honestly didn't know if she could even do it. She left Margret because of the violence and biting humans with no thought to the damage it caused. How could she turn to violence herself? Sure she wanted to learn how to defend herself, but kill someone? The thought alone sent a chill through her body causing her skin to erupt in goosebumps and bile to rise in her throat.

"Isn't there a way to just stop them, without killing them?"

"Mackenzie, I love the fact that you never want to harm anyone. But sweet girl, if you find yourself in a situation to use any of these fighting techniques you've been learning, they won't stop until they kill you. At what point does your life become more important than theirs?"

"I don't know," she whispered, looking anywhere but at the men standing in front of her. Could she do it? Kill someone to save herself? Would she ever be able to live with herself if she did? She had killed before, but she had no memory of it. She just had the bloody evidence she woke to the morning after to haunt her.

"If you are not up to fight, then you tell me now. I will find a safe house for you. Somewhere that Margret will never find you. If you cannot commit to defending yourself in the same manner you are attacked in, then you shouldn't be fighting at all. I won't lose you again, Mackenzie."

She could see the love and concern in her father's eyes. Liam watched the two of them, but he too watched her with more emotion than she would care to see, at the moment.

"She can do it. She doesn't realize she can yet, but Mackenzie is a strong woman." Geoff's voice startled her. Turning around quickly, she saw his strong frame stride toward her and her father. They hadn't spoken since the night before when he practically accused her father of ill intent and sang Margret's praises. Geoff's penetrating stare locked with Mackenzie's eyes as he approached. Her heart started to race, and she knew that he was going to apologize. "Can we talk?"

Mackenzie just nodded and when he reached his hand out toward hers, she didn't hesitate. She laced her fingers through his and followed him as he led her away from the group.

"I screwed up. I was speaking out of my ass. You were right. I was wrong. Does that cover it?" Geoff had a cocky little grin on his face as he spoke and played with her fingers resting in his. He slowly stroked each of her digits from the top to the bottom before running his thumb along her palm and the inside of her wrist.

"How about, I'm sorry?" She knew that she should still be irritated with him. But when he looked at her with those deep eyes and touched her in such an innocent way that still managed to drive her crazy, she just couldn't be. She gave him just a little coy smile back, letting him know that he was forgiven. This time.

"I'm sorry."

"Thank you." Mackenzie went to take a step back to return to her lesson with her father and Liam, but a sharp tug on her hand brought her right into Geoff's arms. His warmth radiated through her clothing and seeped straight into her skin. Geoff released her hand and slid his own around her side and up her back, holding her firmly against his hard chest. Slowly, he lowered his head to her neck and placed a feather soft kiss just below her ear. A shudder ran through her as his nose traced the shell of her ear, and his warm breath whispered over her skin. "Kiss me, Mackenzie," he whispered, then kissed the tip of her ear, letting his tongue linger.

Turning her head, she captured his mouth with her own. His tongue dipped into her open mouth, welcoming him in. She never fought for dominance. This was his. His hands returned to her hips, griping them firmly, pulling her aching body into his. His tongue never yielded, searching out every corner of her mouth as she massaged his with her own. Mackenzie's hands found purchase in his hair, and the two melded together as one.

Finally slowing, Geoff began to lay soft kisses upon her lips, her nose, and finally her eye lids. When she felt his lips recede, she opened her eyes to see a smiling Geoff looking down at her.

"God, I've missed that," Geoff whispered. Mackenzie just nodded in agreement. She didn't want to speak or to move. As long as she stayed right there in his arms, she could pretend they were in their own little bubble, away from Werewolf politics, her long lost father, or the other man that held part of her heart.

~*~

It took Mackenzie and Geoff a few minutes to extricate themselves from one another's arms. When they returned back to the training area, Liam had Darren pinned to the ground, with his legs wrapped around Darren's waist. Liam's arm was wrapped around her father's neck and locked together with his elbow. Daddy dearest looked to be turning a little red.

Liam's eyes were wild as he watched Mackenzie and Geoff walk back. She could see the fire in them as she approached, and she instantly felt guilty for hurting him the way she had. Her father gripped Liam's shoulder and pulled him so fast that his legs and arms flailed out in shock. His body slammed to the floor.

Mackenzie stopped in her tracks as she saw her father standing over Liam's prone body attempting to heal from the blow to the ground. The grimace on his face told her everything she needed to know. Liam was hurt and her father did it.

Running as fast as she could, she threw herself to the ground in front of Liam. The rage she saw on her father's face scared her. She had never seen him look so angry in all her life. Not that he had been in her life very long.

"Mackenzie. Move. Now."

"No. You can control yourself. He can't! Please, Daddy. Calm down. Count to ten or a thousand, I don't care. But figure it out and calm down."

Darren was visibly shaking. His breaths started to slow and increase in depth. Liam groaned behind her, but she wouldn't turn away. After a moment, all tension in her father was gone, and he dropped to his knees.

"Even I lose my cool sometimes. Mackenzie, Liam, I am sorry."

"Not your fault. I started it. I lost control. Again." Liam's voice was angry. She knew that he was angry with her. Her eyes pleaded with her father for a moment to speak with Liam. The grim smile and slight nod of his head told her he understood, and when he stood to walk away, taking Geoff with him, she turned to Liam.

"I didn't mean to hurt you. You know how I feel about you. And him. This is so hard, and I don't know how to handle it when my emotions get away from me." She was pleading with him. She didn't want to lose him. She needed Liam. He had become her best friend. A best friend that she knew she felt more for. A best friend that she knew felt more for her. But she couldn't deny her intense attraction to Geoff. Even if half the time she wanted to bite his head off.

"Don't. You keep saying that you can't pick. That you don't want to do anything to hurt the other. But it seems that is all you're doing. You are stringing us along. I'm getting tired of it. I want you Mackenzie. I want you and no one else, and the fact that you can't say the same hurts. The fact that the person who is holding you back has lied to you and manipulated you, and yet, you refuse to see it. When you realize what you have right in front of you, come talk to me."

He didn't let her respond. He stood up and walked away leaving her sitting in the dirt, tears streaking down her face, and a heavy feeling in her heart.

~*~

It took four days. Four days until Liam showed up to a training that Mackenzie was at. Four days without a single word spoken between the two. Mackenzie felt like her heart was shattering into a thousand pieces.

His long purposeful stride, and gaze that never touched her, spoke volumes. He wasn't here for her. She had lost him. She should be glad that he chose for her, shouldn't she? But she wasn't. She wasn't glad at all. She missed him. Even though he was so close she could reach out and touch him, she missed him.

Geoff had been at every training Mackenzie was at. He helped her when he was needed, always letting his hands linger a moment longer than necessary. What would have thrilled her days prior, felt almost empty. She was having a hard time controlling the deep sorrowful emotions that were coursing through her.

Training wasn't going well either. She couldn't concentrate. Her mind was on Liam, and if he would come and work with her, or if he were working with someone else, or if he were learning what he needed to protect himself. Her father and Geoff hadn't been much help. The constant yelling and growling only irritated her instead of encouraged her. Seeing Liam walking into her training, even if he wouldn't look at her, was the first jolt of motivation she had had since he left her sitting in the dirt.

"Are you ready to work?" Darren asked Liam. With a stiff nod of his head, he took his position beside Mackenzie.

"Are you going to talk to me?" she whispered. She knew the answer, but she had to ask anyway.

His silence was answer enough. The only thing that came out of his mouth in the next two hours was the grunts and groans of sparing.

"I want to work on changing on command," Liam told her father as they were walking back toward the houses. "I want to be as strong and as in control as the rest of the damn wolves coming after us."

Mackenzie knew that she should be focusing on what her father was saying, but all she could think about was the fact Liam said us. The damn wolves coming after us. He wasn't going to leave.

"Earth to Mackenzie?" Liam stood in front of her. His normally sweet and welcoming eyes held an edge to them she had only seen right after he was turned... and up until he cycled the first time. She was certain then, too, that he would never forgive her, but he had. Could this be the same?

"Sorry," Mackenzie said as she rocked side to side slightly, not quite sure what to do or say. Slowly, she lifted her head to capture his eyes with her own. His yellow green irises shone brightly. His blonde hair had grown significantly since they had met, since she had bit him. It used to be kept short, but now it fell over his forehead and into his eyes. With one hand he reached up and pushed it all back, but he didn't look away.

"Did you hear what he said? We are going to practice changing tonight when the moon rises. It's not a full moon, but it will be easier than during the day time. Are you free or do you have plans?" His voice took a sharp edge and Mackenzie was confused. She didn't understand why he would think she had plans that he didn't. Their lives consisted of the camp fire, bed, and training.

"Of course I'm free. I'll be here." Liam nodded his head and walked away. When he got to the edge of the clearing, he looked back at her over his shoulder, and then stepped into the trees.

FOURTEEN

"STOP FIGHTING IT! GIVE IN TO THE WOLF! I can smell it trying to come out. Stop thinking and let it!" her father yelled out from thirty feet away. He said he needed to stand away from them. If he were close, it would be harder to commune with nature or some shit. She didn't really get it since her and Liam stood side-by-side, completely naked, and attempting to shift their human bodies into wolfy ones.

It took every ounce of self-control not to turn and stare at Liam. Mackenzie had seen him nude before, they all had seen each other at one point or another. Nudity is nothing to werewolves. It is a fact of life unless you had unlimited amount of clothing to tear through or only turned on the full moon when you were completely alone. She didn't have any money to really speak of, and screw being alone.

"I'M TRYING! BUT THE BITCH APPARENTLY DOESN'T WANT TO COME OUT!" she yelled back. Liam's strong and silent front was broken. He let out a hearty laugh causing Mackenzie to cut a glance in his direction. Seeing his smiling face—not to mention killer body—happy and laughing because of something she did was enough to put a smile on her own face.

Just like that, the tension between the two dissipated. She knew she still had some apologizing to do, but at least her best friend was back.

"Okay, okay, again," her father said between chuckles.

This time, Mackenzie could feel her wolf inside of her, begging to be freed. She could feel the warmth start in the core of her stomach and spread like wildfire to the tips of her fingers and toes in rapid succession. Muscles and bones begged to be stretched and moved. The scent wafting from the trees and the earth beneath her feet begged her to give in.

Looking over to Liam, she could see that he too was welcoming the beast. Mackenzie gave in and let out a cry of pain as her bones and muscles ripped and broke and popped in two back into place. On all fours. She had done it.

Mackenzie-Wolf spotted another directly in front of her. She could smell him. His alluring deep musky scent. His coat shook and his body tensed. The white fur shone under the moonlight beneath the cloudless sky. She wanted him.

His eyes captured her, a growl resounded from his chest and the vibrations sent chills through her body.

Mackenzie-wolf and the male before her stalked toward one another. Her hackles raised, and she lowered her front to the ground, displaying her rear in the air in offering.

STOP THAT

She knew that voice. Mackenzie-Wolf started to lower herself. Her body still screamed for the wolf in front of her, but she had to listen. Or did she? A growl erupted from her, and she shook her head violently, trying to rid the intruder in her mind.

The male in front of her paced back and forth, eyeing her. Letting out little growls and tossing his head back just slightly. She lowered her whole body to the ground, giving herself over to him. He pounced.

His body collided with hers, and he bit down on her neck, warm and strong.

A pain shot through her, crying out in pain, her muscles contracted and wouldn't release. The white wolf above her body began to spasm and fell to the ground beside her, a whimper escaping his muzzle. Then the world went black.

The world came into view through many rapid blinks of Mackenzie's eyes. Looking around her, and at how close Liam lay beside her, she remembered. They had done it! They had changed without the force of the full moon! But for how long?

"Liam!" She shook him excitedly. "Liam! Wake up! We did it! We did it!"

His eyes shot open and his body tensed. When he looked around and was satisfied there was no danger, he looked to Mackenzie. "We did it?"

"YES!" Without thinking she threw her arms around him and hugged him in celebration. His warm scent filled her nose and images of her wolf-self flooded her memory. Her body went rigid when she felt the heat travel to her nether regions from the mixed stimuli of her naked body pressed against his, and the memory of giving him complete control over her. Wolf form or not, she knew what she was asking for.

Liam pulled back slightly, and looked her straight in the eyes. "This is your chance to get up and walk away. This is your chance. You stay here in my arms, and as far as I'm concerned, that means you chose me."

Her mind raced. This was it. She had to choose. If she got up and left, that was it. She was choosing Geoff. If she stayed, she was choosing Liam. She didn't know what to do. Her heart broke with either decision. She could see the determination in Liam's eyes, and feel his love for her in every touch. She knew that he would be good to her, good for her. But there was something about Geoff she needed to figure out.

Darren chose that minute to make himself known. He strolled over with a look of sheer pride on his face. The interruption of her father caused both her and Liam to move quickly, both grabbing their clothing and dressing. She would have more time to decide after all. She would have to thank her father for that later.

"Well done, you two! Do you have memories of what happened?"

Mackenzie's face flushed after realizing that he had to have seen the display. He was at the tree line, giving them a chance to concentrate while still being close enough to help. Liam smiled a little, and looked directly at Mackenzie and nodded.

"I don't remember everything, but I remember the brindle fur and wild hungry eyes."

Darren cleared his throat and shook his head.

"I think that's good for tonight. Perhaps tomorrow night you will be able to hold onto the wolf for longer than a few minutes. Liam, if you will excuse me and my daughter? I would like a chance to talk with her privately."

"Of course, sir. Thank you again for all the help you have been giving us." With a nod of his head, her father acknowledged Liam's statement, and dismissed him at the same time.

When they could no longer see Liam's retreating form, her father turned to her with a smile.

"You love him."

"I know I care for him deeply. I know that I have been miserable these last few days without him speaking to me. But I don't love him. Not yet. If I loved him, I wouldn't feel so strongly for Geoff. When Geoff is around, I turn to goo. He makes me so angry and drives me crazy, but at the same time, I can't get enough of him. Liam and I are different."

"Can I be honest with you?"

"That's all I ever want."

"I don't trust Geoff."

"He doesn't trust you either."

"I know. I also know he holds a piece of your heart. But if you think about it, really think about it, who have you mourned the loss of more? Geoff when he left without a word or Liam when he told you exactly why he was pulling away? Who do you feel more connection to? Not just physically, but emotionally? Who would you trust with your life?"

"Both of them. Geoff saved me. He found me, granted Margret and Analise were with him, but he found me when I needed someone. He helped me after I... after my first big mistake as a wolf. He didn't judge me and wouldn't let me judge myself. I don't know what I would have done without him. He left his pack to go with me, to protect me and help me figure out what the fuck I am doing. He left his pack to follow the girl who couldn't even promise him her whole heart. That is loyalty. Liam. God, with Liam it's so damn hard. I turned him. I am his sire and from what I've been told, that right there could be the exact reason we feel the way we do. The connection we have could be one hundred percent bullshit."

"I can't tell you who to choose, but I can tell you the sire bond has *nothing* to do with romantic feelings. Not one bit. How do you feel about the Were who turned you?"

"But that's different. He left me there to die. He wasn't my sire, just my attacker."

"His DNA runs with yours now, no matter how he has acted since he bit you. That changes nothing. If I ever find him, he will pay for what he did to you, but what you call a sire bond would still affect you if it were a real thing. Many Werewolves have said that the Sire and the bitten were bound together, but it had more to do with teaching them the way of our life. After so many years together, between opposite sexes, there is bound to be a physical connection."

His words hit her like a wrecking ball. How had she not realized that before? She was a Harvard student, for crying out loud. Or she was. She was a smart woman. Why had logic on this topic alone gotten thrown out the window? She tried to remember who had told her about the sire bond first. Had it been Teresa or Natalie? Or had it been Margret? She couldn't remember who mentioned it first, but she knew for a fact that Geoff had mentioned it since. And quite often.

"So, this pull to Liam, this heart ache when he's away from me, has nothing to do with the fact that I bit him? This is one hundred percent real, not bull shit?"

"One hundred percent real." Her father was smiling at her in that fatherly way. The way that Dad's look at daughters when they see a moment where their little girl isn't so little anymore.

"And Geoff? How do I walk away from him? How can I say I love either of them if I have thoughts and feelings for another man? Daddy, I am so confused."

Mackenzie got close to her father and hugged him for the first time since their talk by the lake. With her arms wrapped around him, he held her tight. She felt safe from everything. From Margret and from herself.

She had to choose, and she knew that no matter the decision, someone would get hurt.

"I know. But you will know when the time comes who to trust your heart with. It will become clear."

Mackenzie thought about everything that had happened in the last few months. She thought about every fight and every stolen kiss she experienced with two amazing men. Then she thought about when they left her. She only shed a tear for one. She knew what she needed to do, but actually doing it was the hard part.

FIFTEEN

The fire crackled loudly as Mackenzie watched the flames dance along the logs in the pit, before devouring them entirely, leaving only piles of ash behind. She was growing more and more comfortable with her father's pack, and she could tell that Geoff was not.

He would constantly jump at the slightest sound or go on walks alone. The only time he seemed at peace was when they were together. When he was sitting right beside her, finding ways to touch her skin. A slight brush of his hand against hers, or sitting so close his foot rested beside hers. All it did was send shivers through her body and guilt through her heart.

She needed to talk to him. To explain that she cared about him, but she realized she loved Liam. She knew it would crush him. Call her chicken, that was fine. She just couldn't find the nerve to break his heart.

"Walk with me?" Geoff whispered into her ear. She was so lost in her thoughts she hadn't noticed his approach and jumped ten feet in the air. His arms circled her waist, keeping her on her feet. "I know I'm charming, but you don't literally have to fall for me."

Mackenzie saw the smug little grin on his face. That absolutely gorgeous face that held her captivated and made her girly bits tingle. That face she was going to crush. She was such a bitch.

"Haha. Let's go this way." Nodding her head in the direction toward the woods, they set off. Mackenzie looked back at the fire, and on just the other side of the flames stood Liam. He watched them retreat with a steely glare, and Mackenzie knew the moment she got back, she had to talk to him.

"Come on slow poke," Geoff said teasingly, tugging on her hand.

"I am! You just have giant man legs. My lady legs don't have that long of a stride."

"Then run. We both know you can run circles around me."

"That's true." She grinned at him. This she liked. It felt easy and fun. Geoff was one of her best friends, and she didn't want to lose that.

He reached out for her. His finger softly tailed down the back of her hand before entwining with hers. They weren't holding hands exactly, but the meaning was still there. For the first time since they met, the physical contact made her uncomfortable. She felt like she was leading him on.

Ahead of them, the trees rustled loudly and heavy footfalls echoed through the area. Geoff and

Mackenzie were on high alert as three large men came bounding through the tree line and toward camp. Recognition of their faces flashed through her mind as some of the men from around her father's camp fire that very first night they found him.

"Come on!" Mackenzie yelled at Geoff as she pulled her hand from his and ran after the men. Something was going on, and from their sudden approach, something not so good.

She heard a few mumbled curses coming from behind her, but Geoff did follow. Even if he didn't really want to.

~*~

"Darren! DARREN!" One of the men called out. His voice was deep and his breath labored. Mackenzie knew how much it took to make a Were out of breath. He had to have been running long and hard.

Mackenzie came to a stop just behind the men. She saw her father's front door open, and Nadia stick her head out. "He will be right there," she called back.

The commotion had called the attention of the rest of the pack. Many had come out of their homes to stand around and watch. The rest were sitting inside by their windows with the curtains pulled back, looking anywhere but at the gathering circle. It was as if they were trying to pretend to not really be interested in anything other than the trees.

Mackenzie's father came out of the house in a fast paced walk. He wouldn't run, and Mackenzie could only guess that it was to keep the others from getting worried because everything in her told her to run. It had to be important.

He stood before the men, tall and strong. She saw him as their leader. She saw the strength and wisdom exuding off him. She smiled slightly, and then remembered something was very wrong.

"The pack to the North, sir," a big man with a bushy beard said so quiet it was barely audible from her position directly behind them.

"What about them, Ben?" her father asked in the same hushed tones.

"Gone."

"Go into my house. I will be right there." Her father dismissed the men, one of which was apparently named Ben, and stayed standing there, facing her and everyone who gathered behind her.

"I will find out what is going on. Do not worry, we have always been led by decedents of Emily, daughter of Merideth, and we always will. I will not let anything happen to our pack. I give you all my word."

Then he turned his attention to Mackenzie. "You three, come with me."

Whipping her head around Mackenzie noticed that Geoff and Liam had come to stand behind her. They nodded to her father and walked on past her without a word. Sighing she followed behind. Apparently, her love life would have to wait a little longer.

She could feel the eyes of her father's pack on her back. She didn't like it. She wanted to turn around and flip them all off, but doing so would only make things worse. She didn't think it was possible for things to get worse until then.

Stepping through the doorway into her father's house felt like a reprieve from his pack. Until the silence in the room fell heavy on her. The men were staring her down with a silent accusation. Darting her eyes to Geoff, for just a brief moment, she saw something that looked like guilt. Quickly, his face was a mask of concern, and he too began looking between everyone.

"Tell me." Her father's voice broke the silence in a deep timber. He was using his pack leader voice. Mackenzie had only been there a short time, but she could already tell the difference in how he spoke in different situations.

"We went out scouting, like you said. We found Genevia's pack and told them what we had heard. She sends her regards and her gratitude for the warning. When we traveled North to find Leona's pack, all we found were bodies. Warm buried bodies."

"How many? Does Leona still live?"

"We did not find Leona. We checked each shallow grave. It is our hope that she got the rest of her pack to safety."

As Ben spoke to her father, the other two kept a close eye on her, Liam, and Geoff. She sent a glare at them in hopes they would realize she could see the hatred in their stare, but all they did was glare back. If her father thought she would be welcomed back one day to lead, she was sure he was mistaken.

"Do not look at my daughter that way," her father's voice boomed. Red flushed Ben's face and his eyes were narrowed. She knew that look. That was the 'oh shit, I'm in trouble look'. Only, the last time she had seen it, it was directed at her when she was snooping around her father's shop when she was a small child.

"Sir, with all due respect, none of this occurred before she arrived."

"With all due respect, screw you," Mackenzie retorted before she could find the filter that should be connected to her mouth.

"That is enough! My daughter did not do this. She left that pack to warn us, to warn everyone. This could be completely coincidental. Margret was already attacking packs and taking over."

"We should be ready just in case our location has been compromised."

Liam was quiet during the whole conversation. Mackenzie could see the concentration in his eyes as he followed along. She could also see him glance to Geoff every few moments and look away quickly. She took a step toward him, hoping to catch his eye. She wanted to know what he was thinking and hoped he would get her silent question. He didn't.

"I think we should wait until after the next moon and then the three of us should go and warn as many others as we can." His statement was loud. It had to be to talk over the others who began arguing over how and when Margret would attack the pack.

"Why after the moon? Why not leave immediately?" Mackenzie asked. Liam looked to her and locked eyes. A silent promise to explain later.

"Why not? This way we can get some more training in, and we know we will be somewhere safe to turn." Liam looked to her and locked eyes.

"I think that's a good idea. It will give us time to plan out our route, and with Darren's help, we can find other packs close to here that much easier," Geoff said.

Mackenzie didn't know what was really going on with the boys, but she couldn't find any fault in their reasons. Maybe after she talked with Liam she would understand better.

"If that's settled, I need to excuse myself. Mac, I'll be back by dinner. I just need some time to process this." Geoff left the house, leaving Mackenzie with Liam, her father, and his three men.

She knew that all this talk about Margret had to be hurting him. She knew he needed time to think and to cope. She would give it to him.

"I think with the moon approaching in the next few days, we should have a family feast. No talk of what is to come, just enjoying the moment with those we love. Perhaps if the children are caught up with their schooling, they can be brought down."

It would be nice to finally meet her little sister. That put a smile on Mackenzie's face. She wasn't an only child. She had a sister. She hadn't even met her yet, but she could feel the blossoms of love for the girl already forming.

~*~

Her father announced to the pack that there would be a family feast that night. A few members grumbled about it not being a time for celebration, but most went along with the plan happily. If there is one thing that can help bring people together, it is typically food.

Darren jumped into the pack's jeep to head into town to check on the pack children and left the rest of the preparations to those still there. Mackenzie offered to help out, but no one really seemed all that interested in her company.

"Don't worry about them," Nadia said, bumping her shoulder as she walked by. "Come, help me catch some fish to cook."

Mackenzie followed along happy to have someone not treating her like Death was following her around, taking out anyone she passed.

"They all hate me, don't they?"

"They don't hate. They are worried and are listening to some fools who would be next in line should your father pass before Lyla is old enough to rule. Ignore them. They will all see. You will do great things, Mackenzie. You and Liam both."

"What about Geoff? He is with us."

"Right, Geoff, too."

Mackenzie wanted to press the conversation further, but Nadia cast her line and began an intricate lesson on fishing.

When they arrived back at the camp with more than thirty fish, four of which Mackenzie was proud to say she caught herself, they found the fire roaring, music playing and people dancing about. Wonderful scents of roasting vegetables and pork filled the air causing her stomach to growl loudly in response. Both girls laughed and brought the fish to the men cooking before wandering about, talking to pack members.

Nadia would include Mackenzie in the conversations, but most of the pack ignored her presence. Finally, Mackenzie was tired of the treatment and excused herself to sit with Geoff and Liam.

"This is stupid. Why would they think I was telling Margret to attack these packs. We hadn't even come across them yet! I wonder if that pack with the jack ass sexist leader is still standing." She was grumbling as she sat down. It had been a hell of an afternoon, and she just wanted it to be over. At least she might get to meet her sister.

Or not. Her father returned in the Jeep without anyone accompanying him.

"Don't worry. You will meet her soon enough." Liam squeezed her arm before standing up and walking over to help stoke the fire.

"We need to make a plan after dinner. Tomorrow at the latest. The moon is in two days time. We need to know where we are going," Geoff spoke softly. She didn't want to think about all the problems going on. She wanted one night with her family, both the one she lost growing up with a mother who kept them apart, and the one she had found in Liam and Geoff.

"I know, but for now, can we just eat and dance and pretend like it's a happy day?"

"Sure, Mac. Anything for you." Geoff leaned over, grabbed her hand, and brushed his lips across her cheek. His stubble had grown out to a modest length and no longer scratched at her skin. It didn't send goose bumps up her skin any more. Closing her eyes and swallowing hard to keep the silent sob to herself, she said goodbye to the feelings she had been harboring for Geoff. She hoped after everything was said and done, he would still want to be her friend.

SIXTEEN

The call of nature the day of the full moon had been just as strong as always, but being there, able to dig her toes in the dirt and smell the leaves on the trees from sun up to sun down had made the day actually pretty enjoyable.

Liam and her father disappeared early in the morning for some one-on-one training, allowing Geoff to work with Mackenzie. He was good at pointing out where she needed more work, and never failed to praise her when she accomplished what they had set out to do.

After training, Mackenzie, Liam, Geoff, and Darren had all sat down together and planned out the different paths that were going to be taken. The three of them would head south while Darren would send scouts the other directions. They had gotten names and locations for at least four packs. One of which was another direct decedent of the royal family. They would be good allies to have.

As the sky turned dark, the fire was put out. The entire pack walked as one further into the woods. Mackenzie and the boys followed along taking in the rituals of pack. It was interesting to see the differences. Her father's pack walked silently, not mournfully, but more in reverence. This was a special and sacred night to them. The night they connected with their whole wolf selves. Sure most could change on their own whenever they wanted, but the full moon called to all of them, both born and bitten. It was a magical night that was hard to ignore. Margret's pack treated it like a party. Between the two, she would take quiet respect over loud and wild any day.

There was only a small open expanse near them, so they all gathered close. Seeing so many members was a shock. Those that lived in town, those that traveled, and those that lived at the camp, all came together for the full moon. Mackenzie stood near her father, a connection between them she had only begun to understand, made her smile. She was about to share part of her life that had been drenched in despair with the man she thought had hated her. Only he hadn't. And he understood her. She looked between the three most important men in her life before the moon hit its highest point in the sky, bathing them all in its light.

The unmistakable pops and cracks rang out from the group, a few screamed in pain, but most welcomed it. Mackenzie welcomed it. She knew fighting the wolf only made things worse. She watched as Geoff and

Liam transformed, idly wondering why she had yet to loose consciousness.

Turning to look to her father, she saw his yellow green eyes glowing brightly beneath a dark brindle colored coat, long muzzle, and a strong muscular frame. He stood at least a foot taller than the rest of the wolves. He looked to her, never breaking eye contact. She supposed she should be afraid, but these people knew her and what would they do? Bite her?

It was only when the large black wolf that had been Geoff bumped her side and nodded with his head in a direction away from her did she look down and realize that she had changed. She could also control her mind.

~*~

The white wolf in front of her ran from the group. Mackenzie charged after him, trying to keep him close enough to intervene should she need to, but not so close as to make him turn on her. She had heard stories of the 'babysitter' wolves getting attacked by the pups. She knew she was faster than Liam, but she also knew she was not stronger.

Geoff yips at her and tries to get her to follow him, but she wouldn't. Geoff didn't need her help, Liam did. And no one in the pack was going to help him. They were all still being treated as Pariahs. With a sharp shake of her head, Geoff ran off at full speed, obviously irritated with her.

It took more concentration than she thought possible not to become distracted by the sights and sounds surrounding her. The deer that was a few hundred yards away, or even the rabbit that was emerging from its hole, test her resolve to stick with Liam. They smelled amazing, and she could feel her stomach growling, but Liam was more important. She was surprised he hadn't taken off after the deer. The aroma filling her nose was intoxicating.

That wasn't the scent of a wild animal. When the wolf in front of her turned into a white blur, she knew he caught the scent, too. Racing after him, she did her best to get in front of him, to do whatever it took to keep him from what she knew he desired most, because in all honesty, she wasn't so sure she wanted to stop him. The scent filled her, and made her mouth salivate. Maybe they could share it.

The moment the thought passed through her, it was gone. She wasn't like Margret. She wouldn't risk another human's life no matter how wonderful the scent was.

Mackenzie threw herself on top of Liam. The two wolves tumbled to the ground, their legs moving too fast to catch them. Rolling back and forth, Mackenzie did her best to stop him. But Liam was stronger. Using his back legs, he kicked out, sending Mackenzie flying into a tree. She felt a crack and landed to the ground with a loud whimper. She watched as Liam stood and ran off. All she could do was wait for her back to heal itself and hope she could get to him in time.

~*~

A large shadow blocked the moonlight from Mackenzie's healing body. She looked up to see her father's wolf looking down at her with worried eyes. He whimpered and nudged her, she huffed and stood. She was still sore, but the bones had healed, and she had to find Liam.

Yipping at her father, she took off. She pushed her feet into the ground hard and ran faster than she thought was possible. Finally, when Liam came into view, so did the girl.

Whoever she was had been smart. She had climbed a tree and continued to climb until Liam had no chance of reaching her by jumping alone. He had resolved to ram the tree in an attempt to dislodge her from it. The tree was just to the side of a steep embankment, and with each attempt at moving back to get a harder hit in, Liam loosened the dirt at the edge. The girls' screams were piercing, and they only doubled when she saw Mackenzie and Darren approach.

Mackenzie knew she had to stop Liam. He wouldn't ever forgive himself, or her, if she allowed him to continue. Looking to the sky to see the darkness beginning to show twinges of lightening, she ran until her body slammed into his.

The two wolves tumbled down the embankment, taking hits from stray boulders and trees along the way. Once at the bottom, Liam's wolf charged at Mackenzie. She was sure he was going to attack and braced herself, but he leapt over her. He struggled as his paws kept losing traction in his attempt to get back up to the girl.

Mackenzie growled at him. She was done with this. He needed to stop. If only he could find a way to push himself through his wolf, none of this would be happening. If she had been a normal every day human when she was changed, without some wolf blood already in her, she would be just as aggressive.

Letting out a huff, she chased after him again.

Liam's wolf snarled at her and growled back, his hackles raised. Mackenzie rammed him again, sending the wolf tumbling back from the little progress he had made. With a snap of his jaw, his razor sharp teeth were embedded in Mackenzie's front leg, and she was tumbling with him. With each bump on the way down, she could feel his teeth ripping apart the muscle tissue in her leg.

As soon as they hit the bottom, he lost his grip on her. The muscles and skin fused themselves back together, and Mackenzie stood before Liam, growling and baring her teeth. She didn't want to attack him. She didn't want to hurt him. But if he tried that shit one more time, she would take him down until the sun took them both from their wolf states.

His slow approach, with his body tall and chest puffed out, let her know that he wasn't going to give up. She knew that she would have to fight with him to keep that girl, and her heavenly scented blood, intact. To keep Liam from hating himself.

Instead of waiting to be attacked, Mackenzie leapt. Taking Liam wolf completely off guard, she managed to land right on him, her teeth sinking into his shoulder. A yelp sounded from him and he thrashed about, trying to knock her off him.

Mackenzie just bit down harder and kicked her legs into him, hoping her claws would make contact.

A heavy feeling began to spread from somewhere deep inside of her. Holding her jaw strong in Liam's shoulder was beginning to get harder, and keeping her eyes open seemed impossible.

Darkness turned to light and Mackenzie and Liam both fell to the ground, their wolves fading into their human form. When they awoke, they were covered in dirt and blood.

SEVENTEEN

"What the hell did I do? Whose blood is this?" Liam asked frantically. He began rubbing his skin, trying to get the blood off, but only smeared it instead.

"Calm down. It's my blood. I promise. We fought. It was just me." Mackenzie crawled toward Liam. She began rubbing his upper arms, from his shoulder to his elbow and back again. "It's okay. I promise. I told you I would look out for you, and I did. Try and remember. Try to trace your night starting before the turn and see if maybe you can remember anything."

Liam nodded and closed his eyes. His cheeks would twitch or his eyes would scrunch and Mackenzie knew that he was remembering bits and pieces. Those reactions wouldn't be from frustration over not seeing anything. When his eyes shot open, and he started to search the woods around them, Mackenzie knew he had remembered the girl.

"Where is she? Why did I get so far from you?" His glare in her direction was accusatory. This was her fault. She knew that, but she also knew she stopped him.

"You might not remember all of it, but we fought a lot last night. You did some pretty decent damage. But I did catch up to you. I did stop you. You didn't bite that girl."

"Where is she?" his tone didn't change. It was as if he didn't believe her and that did not sit well with her.

"I don't know where she is. I got your hungry wolf ass away from her and became your chew toy to keep you fucking distracted. I *know* what it's like to go after a person, I've done it. But you didn't get her. You did nothing wrong last night."

Liam's shoulders slumped forward and his chest began to heave. There were no tears streaming down his face or noise escaping his body, but Mackenzie knew that if she were not right there in front of him, he would be crying.

"She was so scared. The look in her eyes when she was in that tree." His voice was just a whisper, but every heart breaking sound pierced right through her heart.

"Come here." Mackenzie opened her arms and Liam fell into them. Rocking back and forth, Mackenzie whispered words of encouragement and forgiveness. It wasn't hers to give, but she knew that the girl never would know what had really happened that night. She spoke words that she wished someone had said to her.

A rustle in the trees behind them let them know they were no longer alone, but neither attempted to move. Mackenzie didn't care that they were both completely naked, covered in blood and dirt and wrapped up in each other. She was doing what she needed for him. No one could make her stop.

Darren stepped through, completely dressed and took in their positions with a smile before turning to give them some form of privacy. He cleared his throat and spoke with a light tone, "The girl is fine. I told her I was a camper and heard her screams. You came close, but never once did you break the skin. She is going to be perfectly okay and live a happy human life. Well, I can't guarantee happy, but definitely human. You two take all the time you need, we will all be back at camp."

Her father left, but only after looking back over his shoulder and giving Mackenzie a big smile and a thumbs up. Apparently, he approved of her choice. Not that she had told anyone who it was.

"See, she is going to live a *human* life." Mackenzie began rubbing his back, as she held him close. She felt his face tuck into the crook of her neck, the stubble on his face from weeks without shaving sent shivers down her spine. When his lips softly connected with the skin just above her collar bone, her nipples puckered against his chest. "Liam," she whispered into his hair.

"I won't make you choose. I just need to feel close to you. I need you, Mackenzie." Liam spoke between soft kisses that trailed up her neck and beneath her ear then back down, ending with a little nip at her skin.

"But I—" She was going to tell him she wanted him, but was silenced by his lips descending on hers. The warmth that radiated from him mixed with the sensation of soft lips and a prickly beard sent her wild. Her body was on high alert, and she wanted nothing more than Liam.

Climbing into his lap, he had full access to every inch of her body. With one hand in her hair holding her tightly against him, he allowed the other to trace every curve of her body. Mackenzie shook uncontrollably as his large hand cupped and kneaded her breast. When his thumb ghosted over her erect nipple, she moaned into his mouth.

Shifting her hips, she brought his very large and quite impressive dick to exactly the right spot. All she had to do was lift her hips and take him in. Grinding against his shaft, he glided between her warm and aching lips, wetting his dick, rubbing his head against her clit in the process. She bucked her hips again and again. His hands left her hair and breast and gripped her hips, helping her to move harder and faster against him, but never lifting her to envelop him in her warmth.

Liam broke this kiss and stared into her eyes as he moved their bodies together. Mackenzie could feel the pressure building within her. Sweat beaded down both of their skin and just as she fell over the orgasmic cliff, he captured her mouth once more, swallowing her cries of pleasure. His body jerked and his hands tightened on her waist as shots of warm wetness coated her stomach.

She fell against his chest, kissing just above his heart. She felt happy and content. Perhaps it had something to do with her post orgasmic haze, but she had a feeling it had more to do with Liam. The fact that he could send her to nirvana without even having sex was just an added bonus.

~*~

"Liam," Mackenzie whispered

"Shh, Let's just hold on right now."

"But, that was—" Mackenzie didn't get to finish her sentence because a loud rustling came from the trees. Someone was coming their way and fast. Jumping up, and immediately missing the warm and closeness of Liam's arms, Mackenzie stood and waited to see who was interrupting.

She could smell him before she saw him. Cut grass and man. Geoff was going to be there in just a minute. Liam's eyes cut from the trees to her and she knew he could smell Geoff, too. Mackenzie sighed, knowing she had to tell Geoff right away. She wasn't going to wait, not after what she and Liam just shared. It was more than the physical, although if he could do that to her without entering her she could only imagine what would happen when they did have sex.

Geoff crossed through the trees and stood before them with a steely look in his eyes. His nose crinkled up and his lips turned into a snarl. He had brought their clothing.

"Here. I think you might need these." Geoff threw their clothes at them, but missed by a mile. He turned around and stormed off, breaking every branch that had the unfortunate fate as to be in his way.

"Shit!" Mackenzie said as she grabbed her clothes from the mud puddle they landed in. She used her bra to clean off the remnants of Liam's orgasm and pulled the rest of her clothes on quickly. She turned to look at Liam who was watching her like a hawk. She needed to let him know she wasn't going anywhere, but she needed to find Geoff and explain. Geoff should know first. He needed to know that she had chosen Liam. She had wished he hadn't found them naked and covered in each other's cum.

"Don't go after him," Liam said, softly.

"I have to." She could see the heart break on Liam's face, and she tried to reach for his hand, to tell him that she was returning to him, but he pulled away. "I will be back."

Mackenzie ran off in the direction that Geoff had gone, leaving Liam behind. She hoped for the last time.

~*~

"Geoff! Wait!" Mackenzie called out after chasing him for a good twenty minutes. He wasn't going anywhere in particular, but running from her. Finally, she decided to end the damn game of cat and mouse and push forward, running faster than he could until she caught up to him.

She grabbed his arm and planted her feet to stop the forward momentum. The anger on Geoff's face was evident; she just wasn't expecting the intensity of it. She dropped her hand from his arm and took a step back. The feral look in his eyes made her keep her distance.

"Wait for what, Mackenzie? Wait for you to really fuck him then fuck me then still play the innocent little girl act? You either know who you want or you don't. You told us both that nothing would happen between us until you made your choice. I don't deal well with liars."

"What do you call our kiss just days ago? I would say that you have benefited from my stupid behavior. You didn't mind it then." She knew she should just tell him. But he was pissing her off. He was right, but she didn't need him throwing it in her face.

"That's different and you know it. Don't start with me. Just don't. Be ready to head out in an hour. We're going West." The fire in his eyes, and the growl in his voice told her to heed his words. She had never had reason to fear him before, and she probably didn't then either, but she took the warning and left him standing in the woods, just as she left Liam.

She knew how she got herself into this problem— what she didn't know was how to get out of it.

EIGHTEEN

Mackenzie returned to the camp grounds expecting to see everyone out and about, but when she approached, it was like the little mini town they built within their camp grounds was deserted. Walking up the door of her father's house, she could hear the giggles of a little girl.

A smile spread on Mackenzie's face as she opened the door to see Lyla sitting in the floor with a box full of dolls in front of her. Her dark hair fell in waves down her back and when she looked up at Mackenzie, the brown eyes that used to be her own stared back at her. There was no mistaking Lyla as her sister.

"Hi! I'm your sister! How cool is that? I have a sister!" the little girl said as she stood up, dropping the dolls to the floor and running over to Mackenzie. When she wrapped her little arms around Mackenzie's legs and squeezed, a full belly laugh escaped both of the girls.

"That is pretty cool. I didn't grow up with anyone else, so I think it's really awesome to know I have you around. I'm Mackenzie."

"Duh. I know my own sister's name! Come play dolls with me!" Mackenzie knew she didn't have much time, but if Lyla wanted to play dolls for a little bit, she would. For all she knew, that could be the last time she saw her sister. At least, if Margret had anything to say about it.

"Of course you do, silly me."

The two sisters then sat on the floor playing with dolls as if there were nothing more important to be doing. As if someone wasn't dead set on taking over their entire race, or more specifically, killing Mackenzie all together.

She could hear her father talking with Nadia in the background. She could practically feel their eyes on them. When she looked up, she was met with two smiling faces. Yes, this was exactly where she should be. When Mackenzie looked again, she saw the love on Nadia's face as she looked at Lyla, and it made her miss her mother. Sure she had a lot of explaining to do and she was furious with her, but she loved her. Hopefully, before Margret managed to sink her teeth in Mackenzie's neck, she would get to talk to her mother again.

~*~

A knock on the door caused them all to jump. Darren walked over and opened it, letting Geoff step through. Mackenzie sought out his eyes, hoping to see a little less anger and was grateful when she did. He gave her a soft smile before turning his attention back to Darren.

"We need to go over the plan once more. Make sure we are all on the same page."

"Shouldn't Liam be here for this conversation then?" Darren asked.

Mackenzie looked up quickly to see Geoff's reaction. Her father didn't notice the slight tightening of the muscles in his arms or the minute shift in his posture, but she did. He did not like that question. Probably because he didn't like the answer.

"I suppose. I will go get him." Geoff turned and stormed out of the house, the door slamming shut behind him.

"Sorry about that," Mackenzie said, placing her doll down and standing up.

"Trouble in paradise, I see."

"Something like that."

A few minutes later, both Liam and Geoff walked through the door. Neither would look at her. She moved to stand directly beside her father, forcing them both to do at least acknowledge her presence.

"Okay, let's go over this one last time before we hit the road. We are going west. You said there were at least three other packs West of here that we will run into."

"Correct. I am sending scouts South and East. When you reach the coast, you head North. Warn as many packs as you can. Tell them I sent you. Tell them Mackenzie is my daughter. That should help you keep safe travels. If you do encounter Margret's wolves, use your skills. Use your training. Mackenzie, Liam, don't shift unless you have to or unless you plan on killing them. The fact that you are ahead of the curve is a huge advantage. They won't be expecting it. They cannot take that information back to Margret."

Mackenzie could have sworn she saw a look pass between Liam and her father. She couldn't tell what it meant, but they were definitely in tune on something, and she was out of the loop.

"Mackenzie, say your goodbyes. Liam and I will be outside. Lyla, Nadia, it was very nice to meet you both." Geoff and Liam stepped outside and Mackenzie turned to face the family she always wanted but never knew she had.

Lyla's eyes overflowed with tears as she launched herself into Mackenzie's open arms. Mackenzie stroked the little girls' hair and down her back, then hugged her close.

"I will be back, I promise. We can spend all the time together you want. Okay?"

"Okay. I love you, Mackenzie!" Lyla squealed through her tears and hugged her even tighter. After a few moments, Mackenzie broke free and turned to Nadia.

"Thank you for being so wonderful. It couldn't be easy having me show up like this. Thank you for making my Dad happy. I hope we get to spend some more time together sometime real soon."

"Me, too." Nadia enveloped her in a hug and pulled back. She smiled at Mackenzie then went to her crying daughter and picked her up. She whispered something in the little girl's ear that made her smile and slowly the tears dried up.

Nadia turned and walked toward the kitchen with Lyla still in her arms. Lyla waved goodbye and Mackenzie walked out the door behind her father.

NINETEEN

The cool air hit Mackenzie as soon as they stepped out of the house. She hadn't noticed before, but the air was no longer frigid. It was cool, but not cold. And it was still early morning. When she looked around, she could see the fresh green of spring taking hold sporadically throughout the trees that lie ahead of them. Perhaps this was a good omen. A change for the better. They no longer would have to trudge through the snow, the cold, and the wet. It would be bright and sunny and wonderful. They were headed West, after all. Doesn't the West coast get all the acclaim for its wondrous weather and happy people?

Liam shook Darren's hand and then pulled him into a man hug. Mackenzie saw Liam's lips move next to her father's ear, but heard nothing. He must have spoken so softly that the only reason Darren could hear it was his super wolf senses. If she hadn't seen Liam speak, she would have missed the exchange completely, because Darren's response was a quick nod of his head. Geoff didn't even seem to notice.

"Geoff, take care of my girl," her father said, holding his hand out to shake. Geoff clasped Darren's hand in his and gave it two solid pumps.

"Always. Sir, would you mind giving me a few minutes of your time before we head out?" Mackenzie looked at Geoff carefully. He was just hurrying her along to leave, but for whatever reason, he wanted to delay leaving all of a sudden now.

"Alright, what do you need?" her father asked.

"Can we speak in private? I would rather not have an audience." Darren nodded his head and led the way back into his house. Mackenzie's interest was definitely peaked, especially after hearing them close yet another door inside the house. She could only assume it was to her father's room.

"What is that about?" Mackenzie asked out loud, not to anyone in particular.

"I was going to ask you the same thing." Mackenzie turned to look at Liam. Really look at him. She could see the conflict in his eyes when he looked at her. She understood why, and she wanted to put his mind at ease. She just wished that her conscious would let her do that without having to break Geoff's heart in the process. After everything they had been through together, and after how much he had helped her since they met, Geoff deserved to hear directly from her how she felt. And he needed to hear it first.

"I don't know what is going on. He was adamant about leaving here soon, and now he is stalling. If he isn't out in a few minutes, I will go in after him."

"Of course you will," Liam mumbled. It was so low Mackenzie almost didn't hear it and that was saying a lot with her hyper sensitive ears. It was like a knife through her heart hearing how much he was hurting.

"Liam," she said, taking a step toward him. Forget telling Geoff first, she couldn't let Liam feel like he wasn't enough a any longer. She reached out and took his hand in hers and brought it to her lips, kissing his knuckles before dropping their hands, still entwined, to their natural resting place. "I need you to know—"

"Mack, I think you might want to come in here." Nadia interrupted her from the door. She turned around to see a look of panic on her step mother's face.

Mackenzie dropped Liam's hand and ran into the house, her confession of love completely forgotten.

~*~

Mackenzie could hear her father long before she could see him. His voice boomed the minute she stepped through the front door.

"You will not talk to me that way! Be aware of your place!"

Having no clue what caused such an outrage, Mackenzie flew into her father's room to see Geoff calmly sitting in a chair by a desk and her father standing before him, chest puffed out and eyes wild.

"I simply said that Mackenzie is to be my mate, and you need to make her aware of that fact. She should not be fooling around with any other wolf. As her father, it is your job to enforce such rules."

It was as if her presence was not even noticed. The two men carried on with their conversation, never once looking up at her in acknowledgement.

"Where do you get off telling me what is or isn't my job as her father? If I didn't think she would hate me for it, I would rip your insolent head from your shoulders right now."

"And that is why your pack is not as strong as either you or they would like. You feel too much. Mackenzie should be my mate. I am strong, I am old, and I come from a pack with a deep root in our history and will ensure that the pack she and I form together continues to live that history forward."

"EXCUSE ME! Who the hell do you think you are? Do I not have a fucking say in this? I am no one's mate. NO ONE. I choose who I will live my life with, not my father. If you haven't figured it out yet, Geoff, I am not too keen on wolf customs or politics. Seems to me that you don't know me as well as you think you do."

Her blood was boiling. Her skin was vibrating, and she had more murderous rage in her in that moment then she could ever remember having. What was this? The year fifteen hundred? People did not do arranged marriages any more did they?

"Mackenzie, we talked about this. You wanted to be my mate before we left Margret's pack. You wanted to be with me. I was merely trying to go about giving you what you, what we, wanted, but it had to be done the proper way for our kind. A child has to be given if the mother is present to do so. If she isn't, it falls to the father. But he will not abide by our customs and wants you to do so yourself."

His calm demeanor, when she and her father were anything but, set her on edge. How could he be so cavalier with her life? Why would he think that she had chosen him? Was this his way of getting rid of Liam?

"That shouldn't matter. I should matter. What about what I think? What I feel about these stupid customs that, by the way, I never grew up with, so they are worth nothing to me. And how do you propose we grow this pack you want us to start? I can't have kids. Margret making that stupid forest ranger wolf bite me settled that once and for all. Are we going to go around and build a pack, one bite at a time? The *exact* thing we are trying to stop Margret from doing?"

"Of course not. I would create pups with a born that we convince to join our pack. It would be purely for procreation, and you could even monitor the interactions. Mackenzie, don't you get it? I love you. I want us to work, and I am honestly tired of seeing you with another man. I am sure he is, too. It's not fair to lead him on."

"FUCK YOU, GEOFF! What makes you think I would ever agree to bullshit like that? What makes you think I am leading Liam on?" Mackenzie strode across the room to stand in front of the man she had once felt was the answer to her every need. Her fingers closed in on themselves, forming a tight ball and before she knew what she was doing, her arm pulled back and shot forward, landing directly on Geoff's nose. Spurts of blood came pouring out, and for the first time since their whole interaction started, he lost his cool.

Geoff's skin began to vibrate, and his eyes began to turn from his deep brown to the yellow green Mackenzie had grown so accustomed to seeing on herself and all the other bittens around her. When a snarl left his lips, Mackenzie knew he was about to let his anger take over and let his wolf out.

Mackenzie, not able to focus on forcing her own change, felt her legs backing up before she knew she was doing it. Fear held her in place as she watched the man she thought she could love barely hold himself together.

Darren placed himself between Mackenzie and Geoff in the tiny room. His own body vibrating, and a growl was emitting from his chest. One of them had to calm down or they would all have a problem. The door opened behind her and two strong hands gripped her around her waist, pulling her out of the bedroom. The motion was so quick and startling, she jumped. Flipping her body around, she came chest to chest with a very worried Liam. His arms wrapped around her and held on tightly. She was safe.

The door closed quickly behind her. When she turned to see who had helped Liam get her out of that room, she saw Nadia with a worried expression of her own. Only she was watching the door.

A few more growls erupted from behind the door, but they still sounded much too human to worry about two werewolves battling in the middle of a bedroom.

As the noise behind the door quieted, all the worry that Mackenzie felt subsided, and all she had left in her was anger. The door swung open to reveal her father standing tall and unmarked. He pushed past everyone and left the house, his own strides full of energy that she knew all too well. He was off to release the anger and the tension alone. Nadia gave a sad smile before returning to Lyla's bedroom and closing the door behind her.

When Geoff walked out, Mackenzie saw that his nose had already healed and a look of pure sorrow flooded his features. She would not allow herself to feel badly for him. She was angry, and he needed to apologize. A lot.

"Baby—"

Mackenzie turned and ran. She couldn't hear his pleas. She couldn't hear him speak words of love and kindness and caring to her. She needed to wrap her brain around how quick he was to dismiss her thoughts and feelings before speaking with him. Nothing he said would change her mind about Liam, but she had to decide how much she could trust him, after all. He went behind her back to ask her father to force her to marry him, mate him, whatever the fuck the 'wolf customs' decided. She didn't let anyone tell her what to do. If he really knew her at all, he would know that.

TWENTY

Mackenzie could hear Geoff and Liam behind her. She didn't care. She didn't want to talk to anyone. She was still angry, and she knew that the littlest thing would set her off. Mackenzie took a deep breath, counted to ten and back down to one, even threw some rocks at the trees. None of it helped like it used to. Perhaps she just hadn't been that mad before.

"What the fuck happened in there, Geoff?"

"Mind your own fucking business."

Their back and forth did nothing to help her. What did he do? Oh, he just tried to decide her entire future without even considering talking to her about it. He just basically told her father that she shouldn't be slutting it up by not choosing him.

She knew that not making a decision in the beginning was a bad choice. But every damn time she thought she knew what and who she wanted, something more important came up. And now that she did know, she tried to be nice and do the right thing and tell Geoff first, but he is too busy going behind her back to her father. Just thinking about the whole damn thing pissed her off more.

Mackenzie stopped abruptly and pulled a sapling from the ground. The roots hung from the end, dirt and mud clumping them together. With all her strength, she flung the baby tree back in the direction of the guys. She knew it would never reach them, but damn it, they needed to back off and stop arguing where she could hear them.

"What the fuck, Mac?" Liam shouted back after the tree landed a few feet in front of them. Apparently, she had more strength in her than she thought.

"Just back off. Leave me alone for a bit. I don't need to hear you two bitching at each other when I am trying to get my head on straight so I don't bite off one of yours!"

Mackenzie turned and stomped off. Yes, she felt like a toddler throwing a tantrum, but damn if she didn't need some time alone. A rustle in the trees just behind her forced her to turn, ready to yell at whichever man decided he knew better than her about how she was feeling. What she saw wasn't Geoff or Liam. It was a large grey wolf.

The beast that stood before her snarled, its bared teeth. Saliva dripped as the wolf growled. Mackenzie began backing up, too afraid to look away from the wolf for even a second to see if Geoff and Liam were anywhere to be seen. Why the hell had she told them to back off? She needed them. They needed each other. She could only hope that they hadn't run into anyone themselves.

When her back hit a tree trunk, she knew she had nowhere to run. The grey wolf lunged at her. Mackenzie threw her arm up to cover her face just as the wolf's teeth sank into her forearm. For a brief moment, she didn't register the pain, only the sense of deja-vu.

Memories from the night she was bitten flooded through her and she screamed out. She was stronger than she was before. She knew what was happening and why. She would be damned if she let herself fall victim again.

As the wolf flung its head back and forth, trying desperately to tear her flesh from her body, Mackenzie could feel her own beast begging to be released. She curled her free hand into a fist and began punching the wolf in the temple over and over. She fell to the ground, hoping the wolf would take it as a sign he had the upper hand.

He did.

The wolf moved its body above her and released her arm just enough to bite down again. Mackenzie took that opportunity to wrap her legs tightly around the wolf's body and squeeze, and then used her free arm to push off the ground and flip the two so she was no longer on the bottom.

Then, she let her wolf free. The world went black for only a moment, and when the light shone through her eyes again, she was a wolf.

~*~

Mackenzie could feel a powerful energy coursing through her as she squared off with a very shocked wolf. She could see the surprise in its eyes. Before the grey wolf in front of her had a chance to attack again, Mackenzie lunged.

She sank her own teeth into the wolf's shoulder and used her hind legs to kick it, hoping to throw its balance off. She pulled her head back sharply, never releasing the grip her teeth had. As the flesh and fur fell away from the wolf, it let out a howl. Mackenzie opened her mouth to let the vile piece of her enemy fall from her mouth before lunging again.

This time, the wolf was ready for her. His skill and experience was no match for her. She blinked, and before she knew it, she was on the ground, pinned beneath it. His putrid hot breath washed over her, sending an involuntary shudder through her limbs. She watched it open its mouth and bare its teeth as if it were in slow motion.

She knew she was about to die. She closed her eyes and waited for it. She opened her senses to listen for her two best friends, the men who meant everything to her in one way or another. She wanted to hear Geoff's laugh once more, even though she knew it would never come. She wanted to hear Liam say her name with that breathy voice he always used when he was thinking of their time together. She wished she had gotten up the nerve to call her mother at least once since this whole god damn mess of a paranormal life had started.

Determination then filled her, a white hot anger bubbling up from inside of her, burning the hopeless despair to a crisp. She opened her eyes. She wasn't ready to die. This fucking wolf would not take any of that from her. As if a new found strength flowed through her veins, she kicked up, her hind legs landing squarely in the grey wolf's chest. It went flying and as it landed, it skidded in the dirt, leaving an obvious divot in the ground. Mackenzie jumped to her feet and stalked toward the wolf. She could feel the muscles and tendons sewing themselves back together as she moved. The damage it had done to her was fading.

It was time for her to be the one inflicting pain.

The wolf took a minute to stand. Mackenzie circled it, watching as its hind leg gave way under its weight. It was hurt. Good. It stood again, this time stronger. She could see the healing already beginning to take hold. She couldn't let that happen. She ran full speed at the wolf, knocking into it sending it falling back to the ground again. Letting out a full growl, she bit down as hard as she could into its back. The yelp that followed was music to her ears. She relished in it. The pain she was inflicting was nothing compared to the pain she has had to deal with since she was turned. Margret's wolf would return with a message. You don't fuck with Mackenzie any longer.

A thunder of steps came from behind. Her nose was flooded with scents. More than a dozen wolves were on their way toward her. Friend or foe she couldn't tell. If they weren't on her side, she knew that she was in big trouble.

Releasing the wolf's spine from her mouth, she looked over her shoulder for just a second. Long enough to see that the wolves coming were chasing after two wolves, Liam and Geoff, both of which were covered in blood and limping, and long enough to lose the upper hand in her own battle.

The grey wolf beneath her reached up and locked its jaw on her throat. Mackenzie could feel the tendons ripping, the muscles tearing, and her breath losing its strength. As the wolf pulled her back down to its laying position, she followed, not wanting to pull away for fear of tearing out her own wind pipe.

A whimper tried to escape her. All she could do was lie there and watch as Geoff and Liam fought. Sometimes working together, sometimes alone. Geoff dominated. He tossed wolf after wolf away from him. A few got a bite or two in, but for the most part, Mackenzie guessed the blood covering his fur was not his own. Liam was a different story. Two and three wolves at a time lunged at him. He sustained too many bites to count and when he locked eyes with her as her breath grew more and more shallow, she hoped he knew how much she loved him. His energy was fading just as hers was. Margret had done it. She had stopped them from letting the others know. She had, in a roundabout way, brought them into the world of Werewolves, and was most definitely now taking them out of it.

A loud crack resounded through the trees, and Mackenzie watched as the wolf about to bite Liam fell to the ground. Another and another crack sounded and with each one, a wolf fell to the ground. Someone was shooting a gun.

"Quick, end them before the bullet works its way out!" a female voice shouted. The other wolves all stopped fighting and started charging in the direction of the voice. Whoever was helping them was in danger.

More cracks sounded and more wolves fell. A whimper came from somewhere in the distance, and Mackenzie saw Geoff had bitten down on one of the fallen's necks, separating its head from its body.

Mackenzie closed her eyes. The wolf whose teeth still sat in her neck was very much alive and very much not giving up. The sounds that filled the air around her were beginning to fade, as if she were sinking under water. The growls and whimpers and sounds of tearing flesh would be the last things she would hear before she slipped into nothingness.

TWENTY-ONE

Mackenzie couldn't open her eyes, but she did feel gentle hands stroking her hair and her neck. Hushed voices argued back and forth, but it wasn't until she heard Liam's voice struggling to stay steady that she truly could focus on the words being spoken.

"How was I supposed to know they were tracking us?" Geoff asked in an angry whisper.

"That is a good question. You almost got her killed." Liam's words were louder, and his breath washed over her skin with each word. He was holding her, stroking her.

"How the fuck is this my fault?"

"She may trust you, but I don't. If you cared about Mackenzie at all, you would never have allowed any of this to happen."

"I do care about her. I love her. Can you say the same?"

Mackenzie let out a groan. She wanted them to stop. Hearing Geoff say he loved her broke her heart. She loved him, too, just not how he wanted her to. She couldn't. She loved Liam, but she didn't want the first time she heard those words from Liam to be like that, him talking to someone else about her. She didn't want them fighting about her. They had done enough of that.

"Mackenzie?" Liam and Geoff asked simultaneously.

She opened her eyes slowly. Darkness surrounded them, the only light coming from the brilliant red glow of a fire. Mackenzie tried to sit up, but the effort involved was too much, and she fell back onto Liam.

"Gimme a minute." Her voice came out in a scratchy whisper. Just speaking those few words made her throat feel as if it were being rubbed with sandpaper.

"It's going to take a bit longer than normal to heal. He almost killed you. Your spinal cord was nearly severed," Geoff explained. The fact that she nearly died was not lost on her, but she didn't want to focus on it. She wanted to know why she hadn't died and who had saved them.

"What happened?" she asked, sounding a little more like herself, and speaking was not nearly as painful.

"I finished the wolf I was fighting and got to yours. Geoff grabbed his hind leg in his teeth, and I got his neck. He tried to hold onto you, but when he realized how close he was to losing his own head he let go, and we fought," Liam explained.

Mackenzie's eyes opened wide, and looked around for the wolf. Only when she saw that they were alone, did she relax. Feeling more and more of her strength return, she sat back up and stared into the crackling fire.

"So where are we? And did you find whoever had helped us before the wolves did?"

"Of course they did!" A woman's voice called out from behind. Mackenzie whipped around, a bit faster than was probably smart as the sudden pang in her neck suggested, and saw a tall, blonde, beautiful yellow-green eyed woman making her way to the group with her arms full of fire wood.

"ANALISE!" Mackenzie hadn't seen her friend since her first day in the pack house in Montana. Analise had been sent to the California pack house, but the last anyone had heard she chose to be a lone wolf. Mackenzie couldn't really blame her.

The smile that popped up on both girls faces was almost as bright as the fire itself. Mackenzie was happy to see Analise. She had been so worried about her after hearing that Margret sent the California pack to fight another. Well, Margret said they had been attacked, but after learning what she had about Margret's plan of complete and total domination of their kind, she found that highly unlikely.

"Mac," Analise said and opened her arms wide, waiting for a hug.

"Ana, I don't think—" Geoff attempted, but the look Mackenzie threw his way shut him up. She would stand and she would hug her friend. It took some maneuvering, and her body screamed at her more than once, but she made it to her feet and walked over and embraced her friend.

"I am so glad to see you. I didn't know what to think when Margret told me you left the pack."

"I didn't mean to worry you, but I had had enough of the psycho bitch and her war hungry wolves. I couldn't stick around. No amount of hot surfer boys was worth that."

"Well, I'm glad you showed up when you did. You saved our asses."

"I know," Analise said with a smirk. "So I met the new one. Seems to me you have a way with the Werewolf men."

Mackenzie let out a sigh. She did. She wished she didn't. She still had to talk to Geoff and Liam. She hoped that Liam would still have her. "Can we not talk about that right now?"

"Complicated. Got it. That's what they said."

"So, back on point. What the hell happened?"

"Well, I left but still had ears in the house. When I overheard Margret telling the higher ups in the pack to attack, I flipped out. I stormed in and told her off, then stormed out. But not before convincing a friend to keep me in the loop. You, my dear Mackenzie, have caused quite a stir. Margret promised the wolf that would bring you back, alive or not, second in command, and their choice of mates."

Mackenzie couldn't believe what she was hearing. She knew that Margret had it out for her. After all, Mackenzie was trying to ruin her plan that she had obviously been plotting for at least a hundred years, if not longer. But she never thought that she might have a bounty on her head. Not in money, but in status. That pack had no need for money. Margret had been saving for hundreds of years. The bitch was loaded, and bought her pack anything their hearts desired.

"But how did they find me?" she whispered, looking back to Liam and Geoff who had busied themselves with the fire and some kind of meat on a skewer. She was putting them in danger. It could have just as easily been one of them to be killed in that last fight.

"Same way they kept finding me? At least until I figured out to shoot them in the head. They don't like that much. I don't know, but every time they got an update about where you were, so did I, thanks to my contact. I've been working my way toward you for the last two weeks. I guess you stayed in one place a bit too long this time."

"I guess so."

~*~

Mackenzie needed time to think. She had to get some distance from the group to really think about what her presence meant for the people she cared about most in the world. Getting away was nearly impossible as both men objected to her being alone after the last attack. Analise had agreed to go with her, and once they were away from the guys, gave her the space she needed with a hug and a sad smile.

They would never let her leave. She would have to sneak away. She could sneak away and go directly to Margret. She would fight her, and try to win. She didn't have high hopes for victory, but damn it, she would try.

A stray tear fell from her eye and ran down her cheek. Mackenzie swiped it away quickly, not wanting any evidence of her betrayal. That's what it felt like. Like she was betraying Geoff and Liam. They left everything behind for her, and now, she was leaving them behind. It was to keep them safe, but she knew they wouldn't see it that way.

To think, just days ago she had thought how much things had changed for the better. Mackenzie should have known. Her luck was never that good. The sky was beginning to darken, and she knew if she didn't head back to Analise, then back to the boys, people would start to worry and come looking for her. She wanted one more night with them. One more night with Liam.

Mackenzie turned around and began the long walk back. She hadn't realized it before, but she had wandered off the path for quite some time. As the crickets began to sing their song, and the owls announced their awakening, Mackenzie felt calm. She knew what was going to happen for the first time in a long time. For whatever reason, that made her feel better.

As she approached the large rock she left Analise at, she saw her friend waiting, sitting atop the rock with a fierce expression on her face. Mackenzie slowed her steps before coming to a complete stop. Analise's eyes never left hers, and it was becoming more and more clear that the person she was angry with was her.

"What?"

"Don't do it. Don't fucking do it."

"What are you? How did you know?"

"I know the look you had when we left. I know how long you've been gone, and I know that you look calm and resolved now. It doesn't take a genius to put it all together, especially if you add in your stubborn-ass personality. Do not leave those boys with me in some ill attempt to save us all. Let me tell you something. It won't save us. It will just kill you and make them and me grieve, lose focus, and become an easier target for Margret. Don't fucking do it, Mackenzie."

"You don't know that."

Analise walked forward with a strong stride. When she stood just a foot in front of Mackenzie, a sharp sting across her face and a loud crack filled the air before she knew what was happening. Analise had slapped her!

"What the fuck?" Mac shouted, with one hand to the stinging flesh on her face and the other balled up tightly, ready to strike back.

"Get over yourself, Mac. This is no longer all about you, if it ever was. You may have been picked as special, but who knows if you were the only one. You said yourself that Margret set it up to make sure Liam was bit. Did you ever think that maybe the reason he is progressing as fast as you is that he was special, too? Does he have any wolf blood in him? Did you even think to ask?"

The anger left her body in one fell swoop. She hadn't thought about it. But it made sense. He was able to shift like her. Hell, he was turned after her. That meant he was progressing faster than she was. He had to have some kind of Were blood in him before she bit him.

"I didn't. I mean, it makes sense. Analise you are a fucking genius! What about you? Are you able to do shit you're not supposed to yet?"

"Nope, plain old ordinary bitten wolf. Hence the shotgun. Oh, and silver does nothing. I tried."

Mackenzie had to let out a little laugh. Yet another myth generated by humans to try and alleviate the fears of the public.

"Have you tried? I mean, it took a lot of practice. I started remembering bits and pieces before I was able to turn on command."

"Yup, tried that. But I'm in no big rush to be special. I mean, if I'm a nobody, maybe I have a good chance of being forgotten as long as I stay off Margret's radar."

"Does that mean you're not sticking around?"

"Oh, you can't get rid of me that easy. Besides, who would shoot the fucking wolfs in the head, so you don't get your assed kicked?"

Knowing Analise wasn't going anywhere made her feel better. She couldn't leave. Analise was right, leaving would be selfish.

"So, how will you stay off the radar then?"

"I'll stick to the trees and be all Sniper-like with the gun. They'll never know what hit 'em"

The girls laughed, and retraced their steps to head back to the fire.

"So, whose it gonna be, Geoff or Liam?" Analise asked with a sly smile.

"I haven't told them yet."

"You better hurry up. I don't know how long either is going to wait."

"I know."

"Can you tell me? I mean, it's been a while, and if one is off limits, but the other isn't...."

Mackenzie gave her friend a playful shove, but the jealousy inside her roared to life. She wouldn't tell Analise she had picked Liam. She didn't want to have to watch Geoff with her. Although, as far as she knew, those two despised each other. Perhaps she wasn't as over her feelings as she thought. Perhaps just the thought of Geoff with Analise sending her feelings into a bottomless pit would be exactly how Geoff would feel seeing her and Liam together. How could she knowingly do that to him? She was a horrible person.

"How am I ever going to make this work?"

"I have no clue."

~*~

There were more than two voices coming from their camp ground as the girls approached. They were not happy voices either. Both girls quickened their steps, but tried to remain as silent as possible.

"We are just passing through. I swear. Trying to let others know about a possible attack coming."

Liam's voice was clear and strong. He wasn't intimidated by whoever he was speaking with.

"Who are you, and why should we believe you?" The stranger's voice echoed. It was a woman's voice.

"My name is Liam, that's Geoff. We left behind the pack that is attacking the others. We have information that can help you. Just put down the guns."

The word 'guns' put Mackenzie on high alert. All notions of being quiet were gone, and she was in a full run in a matter of seconds. She could hear Analise curse from behind as she tried to keep up.

Mackenzie flew through the trees in time to see Liam and Geoff being surrounded by a group of women, all of which had guns pointed directly at their heads.

Her sudden appearance surprised the group. They all jumped and the guns left the boys, and fell straight on her. It was then that Geoff jumped up, grabbing the woman who seemed to be leading the whole group around the neck and placing himself behind her.

"Now, put down the damn guns!" he yelled out.

"Do not move. They value that one. He will not harm me if she is in danger." The woman spoke with such confidence and power. She was their leader. There was no question about it any longer. Mackenzie smiled despite the situation. It was an all female pack.

"Liam's right, and so are you. They can keep their guns up while I talk. If you believe me, then you tell your pack to lower their weapons, and Geoff will release you. If you don't, then we pack up and leave right here and now, and won't step foot on your land again."

"Go on. Tell us your story, girl."

So she did. She started at the beginning and went through every scary night, every heart wrenching loss of control, and every happy moment that had happened since she was changed. When she began discussing the Royal Were, and how she fit into the whole mess, the woman in Geoff's grip shuddered. Mackenzie could tell by her reaction she knew of the Royal Were, and it wasn't a happy thought.

"So, you're of royal descent. Darren is your father, granddaughter of Henrietta. Your family line is a strong one. A fair one. Your grandmother helped our pack form. You see, I too am of the royal line. My mother had me with a human, and left me with him when she thought I didn't have the gene. When I turned for the first time, Henrietta found me. Recognized me. Apparently, I look like my mother. Her pack had been taken over, and she had been killed. Henrietta brought me in, and when I was old enough, had enough control, I set out on my own to form a pack that I believed in. A pack of choice. No member of ours has been bitten against their will. Henrietta was a good woman. Your father a good man. Lower the guns."

The women surrounding them all lowered their weapons, and Geoff released their leader. She rubbed her neck and walked to stand near Mackenzie. Geoff and Liam stood close, ready if needed, but trusting in the camaraderie that Mackenzie was able to establish in just a short amount of time.

"Did Henrietta ever tell you more about your mother's pack?" Analise asked, panting from behind. She had finally caught up just as the stand-off ended.

"She did. My mother ruled over Alaska. She had a large expanse of land and a large farm house that held at least twenty wolves. The others were allowed to keep their own homes throughout the state."

Mackenzie's stomach dropped. Alaska. Margret.

"The woman, Margret? She has a pack in Alaska. A large one."

The woman's eyes lit with a fiery rage Mackenzie hadn't seen from in anyone before.

"Where is she?" The woman's words seethed through her teeth. Her skin vibrated with anger, and her eyes flashed the yellow-green that made Mackenzie step back, afraid the woman's wolf was mere seconds from taking over.

"She could be in Montana, Alaska, or California. Or anywhere in between recruiting. We are just trying to give other packs a heads up as we travel."

"Then we too will travel and give warning to other packs. We will find her, and I will avenge my mother."

Mackenzie noticed Geoff stiffen. His face never changed, but she could see the worry in him for Margret. She was really trying to understand his need to cling to the idea of the woman who raised him, but how could he still care for her after everything they had learned? After she sent assassins to kill them all, including him?

The woman and her pack took their leave just as quickly and silently as they came, leaving Mackenzie,

Liam, Geoff, and Analise sitting around the fire staring off after them.

TWENTY-TWO

Analise fell asleep in front of the fire, and Liam stood, pacing behind her. Mackenzie could tell he was deep in thought, but didn't say a word. She didn't want to disturb him. They all had a lot to think about, and she knew when Liam was ready to tell her what was bouncing around in his head, he would.

Geoff walked over and sat down next to her without a word. He leaned over, bumping her shoulder with his. She looked over, not quite knowing what to expect. So much had already happened since they had left her father's camp. She couldn't find it in her to be angry any more. She almost died, he could have died, and he put his life in danger to try and keep her safe from a band of gun wielding women.

"Can we talk?" he asked, softly. Liam's head snapped in their direction for the briefest of moments, before turning back to stare at nothing while he paced.

"Yeah, I think we should."

Geoff stood and held his hand out to her. Slipping her hand into his felt different. She could still see his beauty and feel the strength that exuded from him, but holding his hand no longer sent sparks flying. But the connection to him still felt nice, comforting, safe. With a soft tug, he pulled her to her feet, and the two moved farther from the group, but not so far they couldn't see the fire burning. They learned their lesson earlier. They needed to stick together.

"I was wrong, and I'm sorry. I thought I was losing you. I shouldn't have gone to your father, but it was the first thing that I thought of. Can we blame it on my age?" Mackenzie could tell he was trying to apologize while keeping things light.

"Yeah, old age does tend to make men go senile. What's next? Hair loss?" Perhaps if she could keep the friendly vibe going, it wouldn't be so hard to tell him.

"When this whole mess is over, decide then? I know I'm losing you, Mackenzie. I just want a chance to earn back everything I have lost. Don't choose Liam just yet. I don't think I could stand seeing you together, and right now we need to stick together. Just... give me a little longer? Let's finish what we set out to do, and stop this whole stupid mess. I need you right now, Mac. I know no one cares, but Margret has been my mother for over two hundred years. I am trying to come to terms with not only losing her, but most likely seeing her life end at the end of this. If I lose any hope of you loving me, I don't know if I can stand it."

The jovial tone was gone and all that was left was an almost broken man who's eyes shined with something deep, so deep she didn't want to completely understand it. He needed her, and her intention was never to cut him out. She cared about him deeply, loved him even, just not in the way he wanted. She hoped her friendship would be enough for him, though she doubted it.

"Okay. Come on." Mackenzie started walking back to the fire. She could feel Geoff watching her from behind, and when she looked across the fire, she could see Liam's bright eyes trained on her.

~*~

The sun rose above the trees, sending a cascade of shimmering lights onto the four. The new leaves growing on the trees created a dappled effect that would let the line shine in their eyes, and then moments later, they would be basked in a small shadow. Squinting, Mackenzie sat up.

The chirping birds made her smile. A sure sign of spring was waking to the sound of the birds. It was Geoff who woke after her. He sat up and stared off into the woods, not speaking at all.

After ten long minutes, he spoke.

"Do you forgive him?"

"Who?"

"You're father."

"Once I realized there was very little to forgive, yes. He did leave, but he wasn't the person my mother made him out to be. He left to keep me safe, not that it did a lot of good. He ran for all the same reasons I did. How can I blame him for that?"

"Easy. He could have checked in, or at least wrote letters. He didn't have to be around for that. No way anyone is hurt unless it's a paper cut."

"Do you forgive Margret?" Mackenzie was trying really hard not to let her irritation show.

"I'm not really sure that I have anything to forgive, either. The reason I left wasn't because of Margret, but because of you. Sorry, for you. I left *for* you. I left because you did. She hurt you by giving you the gift of the wolf. I know you don't see it that way, and that's why it hurts you. I know you don't agree with her methods of growing her pack, and I know that you see it as wrong. I never want you to look at me the way you did that day in the clearing again. When Margret told you, us, the plan, I thought the hatred pouring from your eyes would strike my heart dead right then and there. But her methods are a way of the wolves." His voice was low and he wouldn't look at her. With his admission the night before about having a hard time dealing with the idea of losing Margret for good, she knew what made him bring all of that up. But that didn't mean she wouldn't argue the point with him.

"And what about the wolves she keeps sending to kill me? To kill you? The wolves she sent after Analise? Is that just the way of Werewolves? What kind of loving mother sends assassins after her own 'son'?" Mackenzie made air quotes around son. If Geoff wanted to view Margret as his mother, she would go with it. But she couldn't stand the thought of her blood coursing through his veins.

Geoff never answered her. He just sighed and stood, walking off into the trees. Mackenzie knew that she shouldn't let him go far alone, but she needed to calm down. She needed to stop shaking. She was surprised she managed to keep her voice at an even level while talking with him. If he said much else in defense of that stupid horrible woman, she might have snapped.

"That was one interesting conversation," Analise said with a scratchy voice that plagues just about everyone first thing in the morning.

"I don't— I mean— GAH!" Mackenzie was so frustrated she couldn't even get a full thought processed or a sentence out.

Mackenzie stood and began pacing back and forth in front of the now charred wood pieces that still held a few glowing embers. She tried calming herself by breathing deeply and when that didn't work, she thought of their conversation the night before. She thought about how he may joke that his age is the reason behind a lot of his actions, but it truly is. Margret has trained him for over 200 years that Werewolves behaved this way. It would take a lot more than Mackenzie to break him of that thought. Unfortunately, he didn't even have her. Not in the way he wanted. She knew she told him she wouldn't make a decision before all was said and done with Margret, but it was hard to forget the one she already made.

"He'll come around. When he realizes that Margret is a psycho bitch who doesn't care if he lives or dies as long as she dominates the world, he'll come around."

"I don't know if I want him to realize that. I want him to come around, but no one should ever feel like that from someone they considered family. That is the ultimate heartbreak. I don't want to see him hurt."

"He's a big boy, Mac. He will be fine. You just have to let him deal with it. All of it. However he needs to. If he needs to run into the woods to pout or pound a tree, you have to let him and not run after him. He wants you and if in the end, you plan to leave with sleeping beauty over there, you can't keep trying to make him feel better. It means more to him than to you."

Analise was right. Mackenzie knew it, but it didn't make it easier. Geoff was her friend. He was more than just a friend, he was one of her best friends, and they had been through hell and back together in the last few months. Instead of responding, she just nodded her head and sat back down. Mackenzie tilted her head back and watched the sparse clouds float across the sky and waited for Liam to wake, and Geoff to return.

~*~

Liam had woken, and Analise had gone to catch breakfast. Mackenzie was beginning to worry about Geoff. What if another group of wolves found him? It wasn't as if that was such a farfetched idea.

Mackenzie began watching the trees in the direction Geoff had left. Any rustle or sound had her on edge. Analise came back with pieces of a rodent of some sort and a shirt full of berries. Big guns and small animals usually resulted in multiple bits and pieces. Mackenzie looked away with a shudder, and then decided to go looking for Geoff.

"Hey, I'll be back. I want to go take a quick look around for Geoff. Get cooking, I'm hungry!" Analise stuck her tongue out at her and Liam watched her. "I'll be right back, promise." She spoke directly to him. He just nodded his head, and walked over to help Analise restart the fire to cook the meat.

Mackenzie pushed through the thickening trees in search of Geoff. He had been gone for a while. She hadn't meant to set him off, but everything she said was true. He questioned her ability to forgive her father, why shouldn't she question his? Geoff was determined to prove that Margret wasn't as horrible as Mackenzie thought she was, but when the facts were written down, Were-tradition or not, she just couldn't find anything inside her to justify Margret's behavior.

After a while, without a single clue as to which direction Geoff left in, she decided to turn around. He was a better tracker than she was. He would be able to find his way back to camp eventually.

Mackenzie looked around and realized she wasn't really sure which way she came from. Sure she could turn directly around, but she had made so many twists and turns along the way it would be a miracle if she made it back before Liam and Analise had finished eating all the food.

Taking a deep breath in through her nose, Mackenzie tried to locate her own smell. Perhaps it was time to work on those tracking skills. Every few feet she would stop and sniff a tree, or spot a footprint that she matched up against her own sneaker clad foot. After the third turn, when she breathed in, she not only smelled her own scent on the tree, but Geoff. His scent was strong. He was close by.

She had every intention of letting herself be known, but the next words out of his mouth held her frozen in place.

"Mom, I know. We are heading West, like I said. But we ran into a snag. The daughter of the Alaska house we took over? She formed her own pack. It's big and strong, and Mackenzie told her about you. We need to move faster."

TWENTY-THREE

Without thinking her statue like status was thrown out the window. Mackenzie charged forward, not at all silently, to see a very startled Geoff standing before her with a phone she didn't know he even had pressed against his ear.

"I have to go," he said and pulled the phone from his ear slowly, flipping it closed, and put it in his pocket. "Mackenzie, listen—"

"How could you? You back stabbing bastard." Her voice was filled with venom. Memories of little things flooded through her mind. How Geoff would disappear randomly, how he needed time alone, how he kept playing with her heart, pushing her away only to pull her back. Begging for her trust, asking for her as his mate. Even though she didn't want that, she didn't realize she was just a pawn in his game. His and Margret's game.

"Margret is my mother, Mackenzie. How could I turn my back on her?"

"She isn't your mother! She was your pack leader. A vindictive, manipulative, bitch of a pack leader!"

"Do not speak of her in that way. I have had to listen to you and Liam bad mouth her to every fucking Were we have met. Do you know how hard it will be for her now to take over as their leader with any ounce of respect in place? And she is my mother. The letter I told you about that I got telling me what was coming? That was from her. When she found me she told me. Margret is my mother. She has been there for me for the last two hundred and twenty years. Do you really think that anyone is worth breaking that kind of bond?"

"So it was all a lie. Every bit of it?" She hated that her voice quivered. She hated that it mattered to her so much. But it did.

"Not all of it. I never would have let them kill you. I do care about you, Mac. I just needed you to see that you need me. That together we can be stronger than we can apart. You can still be my mate, be by my side when I eventually take over for my mother when her day comes and rule over all the Were's in the world. I love you, Mackenzie. That was no lie."

She couldn't believe what she was hearing. How could he think she would ever go along with that? If she were his mate would she have to? Was there some kind of stupid magical bond that made her obey him as if she had no will of her own? How could he love her if he told Margret—his mother—where to find her? He wouldn't let them kill her, but what about hurting her, or almost killing her, as the case may be. What about Liam and her father's pack and Analise?

"Do you have no sense of right and wrong in that fucked up head of yours? So killing me is pushing it, but almost killing me is fine. Killing Liam and Analise is fine because they don't agree with your fucking plans of global domination. What about my father? His pack, did you tell Margret where to find him?"

"Yes. Of course I do, but damn it, Mackenzie you are still viewing the world as a human. Give into your wolf, and you will see that power is everything and eliminating those who do not conform to your will is the only way to gain the respect of the packs. Your father left you a long time ago. You spent a little time with him, but not much. You will get over it soon enough."

"What the fuck does that mean?"

"It means, that yes. Every pack we have encountered has been reported back. You didn't even know it, but we have been helping Mother, not stopping her. She has acquired three new packs since we left. It is only a matter of time before she finds your father's pack. If he had just given you to me as a mate, his pack would have been considered family, and he would have been given the option to submit. But he didn't and he won't. He is too proud of a man."

A growl ripped through Mackenzie's throat, deep and low. Her skin felt like it was vibrating with a hate so strong she would shed it at any moment. When Geoff's eyes widened at the site of her, they quickly turned Yellow-Green, expecting a fight. Good. He was going to get one.

~*~

Mackenzie dropped to the ground, feeling the earth beneath her hands. She dug her fingers into the dirt, grounding herself with nature and gave into the beast begging to be released. With a few cracks and pops, she had changed.

It didn't hurt nearly as much or take nearly as long as it had in the past. Perhaps time just felt faster, and her anger just masked the pain, but it didn't matter. What did matter was Geoff hadn't changed yet.

He watched her with careful eyes and held his hands up. Perhaps he thought that would stop her from attacking him. Perhaps he needed time to figure out his next move. Either way, it meant nothing to her.

Mackenzie snarled, her fur on end, and leapt. She watched almost in slow motion as she flew through the air, Geoff's human form burst into the large black wolf. The minute she landed on him, her mouth was open and her teeth began snapping. She was trying to latch onto any piece of him she could. She wanted to rip him apart. Literally.

Geoff used his strong hind legs to kick her off. Mackenzie fell back with a thud, her ribs aching where he made contact. He let out a growl of his own before freeing himself from his wolf form and turning back. His clothes were in tatters so he stood before her in the nude. It no longer enticed her. It only served to make her want to wretch at the thought of ever being with him in an intimate way.

"Stop it. You know I will better you each and every time you try. Do not make me be the one to hurt you. I don't want to hurt you."

She wanted to say 'too late'. That what he had done was worse than any physical pain he could have inflicted on her. Instead, she pounced before he could change again and bit down on his shoulder. She could have gotten his throat. She should have. But she didn't.

She tore her mouth from his body without releasing him. Flesh and blood shot out from him along with a pain filled roar. Spitting his flesh to the ground she eyed him. She would not back down; she would not turn and leave.

"You fucking bitch! You will regret this. I could have given you everything," he screamed. He took that moment to turn, and his shoulder healed before the last piece of fur popped out from his skin. He growled loudly at her and ran off.

Everything? Maybe everything except a shred of morals.

~*~

Mackenzie didn't know what to do. How could she go back and tell Liam that he had been right all along? That she should have trusted him. That her stupid attraction to Geoff put them all in danger and killed so many.

She stayed where she was, never changing back, never moving, for what felt like forever. Her body, though still in wolf form, sobbed. She was having a hard time combining the Geoff she just met with the one she had considered one of her best friends. She tried to explain away his betrayal. Perhaps the oath he took to the pack and the bond he had with his mother was clouding his judgment. Maybe he didn't have a choice. No matter how she thought about it, she knew it was a lie. He had fooled her. He used her need for closeness and acceptance against her. It was the last time she would ever allow anyone to do that to her.

Slowly, she stood and padded back to the camp they had made. Liam and Analise were sitting by the fire, eating their breakfast when she approached. Both dropped their food when they saw her wolf approach. Mackenzie gave out a huff before closing her eyes and willing her body to change back.

The change back was hard. It took longer than she thought it would and every bone that cracked and popped into proper place was felt. But she didn't cry out. She was done being hurt by Werewolves, even if it was her own.

"What the hell?" Analise asked as she ran forward. Mackenzie just reached her hand out and pointed to a water bottle that was sitting by her bag. Analise handed her the bottle, and within two seconds, Mackenzie had drained it.

"Clothes. Please," she added on when she realized how rude she was acting. Analise once again provided what she was asking for. Mackenzie dressed quickly and looked up to see Analise watching her intently, and Liam scanning the tree line, his eyes darting back to her every few seconds.

"Geoff. He's gone. He's been working for Margret this whole time."

Mackenzie didn't realize how loud two people could be until the shouting began. If they kept it up, any men that Margret had sent would be able to hear them miles away.

"SHUT THE FUCK UP!" she shouted over the ruckus.

Liam and Analise immediately stopped and stared at her. "We don't know how close they are, and after attacking Geoff like I did, I don't think they will be taking it easy on us anymore."

Mackenzie went through the whole story. Every agonizing detail she wished was just a dream. The pity that fell into Analise's eyes as she spoke about her father's pack was heavy. Liam held no pity. Only shear rage.

"Where did he go?" Liam ground out through his teeth. His muscles were clenching and unclenching under his skin. Mackenzie could hear the speed of his heart, and see the rise and fall of his chest, breathing in deeper than normal. Liam was ready for a fight.

"I don't know."

"Don't fucking lie to me, Mackenzie. Don't protect him anymore. I *told* you we couldn't trust him. But you wouldn't listen. Those packs that fell? That's on you."

His words were like a knife, slicing through her skin, and digging into her stomach before twisting and pulling out, slowly. The worst part was she agreed with him. Mackenzie watched Liam drop to the ground, and change into his beautiful white wolf before running off, disappearing into the trees she had just emerged from.

Sobs racked her body, and as much as she wanted to make things right, she had no clue how. She lost Geoff, if she ever had him, and she was pretty sure she just lost Liam, too.

TWENTY-FOUR

"Should I go after him?" Analise asks in a whisper from beside her. Liam had run off over an hour prior, and Mackenzie had yet to move. Analise had decided to sit with her, and rub her back after the sobs continued on for twenty minutes. The tears were all gone, but that was only because her eyes were so dried out they stung.

"What good would it do? He doesn't want to be here. I should have trusted him. Why couldn't I see what he saw?" Mackenzie's words were scratchy and low. She didn't look at Analise, she couldn't. She couldn't handle anyone feeling bad for her. She did this. She wasn't someone to feel bad for, she was someone to blame.

"Because he was an extremely good liar. Because your heart was involved. Because he was hot as hell, and I bet the two of you had some steamy moments clouding that brain of yours. Whatever the reason, this is on him. Not you."

Mackenzie just nodded. She didn't agree with her, but she knew if she argued the point, it would do no good. "So, what now?"

"Now, we wait for Liam to come back, because he will, and we have a killer plan to try and fix the shit that Geoff has done. And then we eat, because fuck, I'm hungry."

Mackenzie looked up and saw a silly grin on Analise's face. To think, when she first met this girl, she thought she was the biggest bitch in the world. And here she was, doing everything in her power to help Mackenzie, to make her smile, to let her know she isn't alone.

Mackenzie let out a laugh. A maniacal laugh that had no purpose other than to let out everything in her that was bottled up. She held no more tears, but the pain was still there. She held no one in her arms, but the love for both absentee men, even if one didn't deserve it, was still there. But the smile on her friend's face was right before her, and that she could return.

"What creature did you kill this time?" she asked with a grin.

~*~

"Going directly after Margret would never work. We would never get close enough without getting caught," Mackenzie said after the third time Analise decided to bring it up. They had been working on plans since they finished the rodent (whatever it was) for breakfast.

"That's why we sniper her ass. I shoot her in the head then you, Werewolf princess with super speed, run in and kill her while she is already down."

"We would still have to know where she would be, when she would be there, and hope to God that we don't get caught in the mean time. It's not realistic. That's a shotgun, not a sniper rifle. And I may be fast, but they would be protecting her, and my fighting skills are not where they need to be for that."

"But with Liam with you—"

"If he comes back."

"Like I said, with Liam with you, you two shouldn't have an issue."

"We met another pack recently. They seemed to be pretty strong warriors. All women, too. Geoff just told Margret about them. Maybe we can back track and find them. Get them to help? Or at least warn them."

"You mean trust another pack? Haven't we had enough trouble that way?"

"I trust my father and his pack."

"That's different."

"How?"

The trees rustled behind. Both girls jumped to their feet, ready to protect themselves. Mackenzie could feel the wolf just beneath her skin, ready to pounce forward should the need arise. She was beginning to like having her there, her guard dog. She still couldn't accept the wolf was her, even when she was in control. Calling the wolf a her, keeping them separate in her mind, helped her cope.

When Liam stepped through, all the muscles Mackenzie hadn't realized were tensed, relaxed. She was so thankful that he came back, that he was in one piece, and his nude form didn't even register.

Mackenzie stood and ran forward, throwing her arms around him. Feeling his strong body beneath her arms, under her fingers sent a wave of relief through her. His smell invaded her senses, and the tears that had been at bay were no longer contained.

"You came back," she said into the skin of his neck where her head was tucked. It wasn't until then that she realized he wasn't hugging her back. His arms were still to his side, not touching her. She let go quickly and stepped away.

Liam's eyes were sad, and he wouldn't look directly at her. His body didn't stand tall like normal, but instead held a slight slump. He walked passed her without saying a word to gather his clothing.

Watching him move, without so much as a glance her direction, spoke volumes. She had lost him, too. Was he back to collect his things and be on his way?

"Don't look at me like I'm a fucking Ghost, Mackenzie. I'm right here. I'm not going to disappear. But goddamn it, you need to listen to someone other than yourself once in a damn while."

"I'm sorry." It wasn't enough. She knew those two words would never be enough. But she didn't know what else to say. Nothing she could say would bring back the lives she had gotten killed.

"It's not all on you. I could have put my foot down. I could have been more adamant about my gut feeling about him. I could have left at any time. But I couldn't. I wouldn't. You would have ended up with him, listening to every word he said. He would have gone about starting a new pack the same way Margret had, only they would be under her control, and you wouldn't know it until it was too late."

"I should have listened to you."

"Yes, you should have."

"What do we do now?"

"You two kiss and make up, then the three of us sit down and come up with a real plan." Analise's presence had been forgotten until that moment. Maybe that was her problem. When it came to the men in her life, it was as if she was in a bubble and nothing else outside that bubble existed.

"A plan is a good idea." Liam ignored the comment about kissing and making up. It didn't surprise Mac after his reaction, or lack thereof, to her attempted hug.

"Right," she said and walked over to the log by the ashen fire pit and sat down.

~*~

When Analise and Liam sat down near her, Mackenzie looked back and forth between them. They had stayed. Even after she had proved to have no real sense of judgment. Even after knowing that she had lead Geoff straight to a gold mine of packs for Margret. Even knowing that if they stayed with her their lives were in danger. They stayed.

"So, what now? Mac won't let me shoot the bitch in the head. She doesn't think it will work. You got any bright ideas, blondie?"Analise asked Liam.

His eyebrow cocked in question at the nickname, but he didn't say anything about it. He just let out a breath before turning to look at her. "I spoke to your father about my concerns. He agreed with me that there was something off about Geoff. Neither of us had proof and figured if we brought it to you together, you would flip out about it."

Mackenzie knew they were probably right. She defended Geoff left and right. Look where it got her.

"So let me get this straight. You thought you knew Geoff was a trader, and you made a plan to go find *more* packs with her father, and told him about it? Are you fucking crazy?" Analise said

"We lied when we said that your father was sending men to the south and the east. He didn't go anywhere but to their houses in town. They left the compound in the woods, but they did not give Geoff a chance to send men to pick them off. We should go back and find them."

Mackenzie closed her eyes. It was too much. Liam had protected her father's family. He protected her. How could she have ever been unsure of him? She opened her eyes and looked at him through unshed tears. Standing, she moved in front of him, and then knelt down between his legs.

Mackenzie reached up and cupped his face in her hands, holding him steady so he wouldn't look away. Her heart was racing, and she could feel the heat coursing between them.

"Thank you," she said. Without another word passing between them, she leaned in and pressed her lips to his. Perhaps it wasn't the time, but she needed to try and convey all that she felt for him in that moment through that kiss.

At first, his only response was a faster heart beat. Then slowly, the rest of his body caught up. His hands gripped her hips and pulled her closer until their bodies were touching. He opened his mouth and thrust his tongue forward, forcing her mouth to open and wrapped around her own tongue in a sensual dance. The feel of him, hard muscle, pliant lips, and demanding tongue, ignited a fire in her. She allowed her own hands to explore the expanse of his back, starting at his neck and traveling down as far as she could reach without pulling away, then traveled back up to his face, caressing it, asking him to be gentle with her.

It wasn't time for rough and passionate. It was time to tell him how she felt. To express everything she could say with her kiss. His hands loosened until all she could feel was his fingers tracing small lines along her sides, her back, and finally he too, cupped her face. The kiss slowed down, and all that was left was sheer emotion. Mackenzie pulled back, leaving a trail of soft kisses from his lips to his ear where she whispered, "I love you."

TWENTY-FIVE

The reaction Mackenzie had gotten from her admission wasn't what she had hoped for. Liam's eyes widened, and then hardened. He pulled away and began pacing back and forth. Mackenzie looked to Analise, knowing full well she had seen the whole thing and must have heard her. Analise gave her a small, almost sad, smile, and shrugged. She didn't know what he was doing either.

"Um, Liam? Mind filling us in on whatever is flying through your brain right now?" Analise asked. Mackenzie didn't dare say a thing. She didn't want to make it worse.

"I'm thinking we stay right here for the night."

"What? Why? He knows we are here," Mackenzie blurted out. So much for the staying quiet thing.

"Because he knows you would go running off to the last pack we found to warn them. He knows we wouldn't stay where he left us. So we do. We stay put.

He won't send anyone here, because he knows we are too smart to do it. He knows you care too much about others, so you would run off and warn them. So we don't. We protect our own asses, and stay put. At least for tonight."

"But—"

"Damn it, Mackenzie. No buts. We did things your way for so long, and look where it got us. Can you please *try* to trust me?"

"Okay." He had been right before, and none of her choices as of late, had turned out too well. It was time to let someone else take charge.

"Damn it—wait. Okay? You're agreeing that easy?" Liam stopped his pacing and stared at her in shock.

"Damn, Liam. You must have lips of gold to shut her up so quick." Mackenzie shot a smirking Analise a scowl. Forget what she said before. She was still a bitch. But the bitch was her friend, so she would deal with it.

"Well, if we are staying here, I think we need some more food and fire wood. If we split up, we can be back in half the time." Analise raised her gun and wiggled it a bit. Apparently, she was getting the food.

"No, we stay together. We work as a unit. First, the firewood, then the food." Liam was taking charge of everything. Mackenzie wasn't sure why, but all of a sudden, his hottness factor tripled.

"Fine, but can I ask a teeny tiny favor? No more kissy kissy when you know I'm watching? I haven't gotten laid in months. If you two keep carrying on like you just did, I might have to jump in." Analise was most definitely a smart ass.

"No probelm." Liam was quick to respond. Quick to agree with her. What happened?

They all packed up what little belongings they had, and put them in their packs. No sense in leaving anything behind to be found, even if they were returning. Collecting the wood was easy. Trying to hunt with three people lumbering around the woods was a different story all together.

"If either of you make another sound, I might have to shoot you instead of an animal." Analise was irritated. They had been wandering around the woods for three hours. Every time they got close to a meal, either Mackenzie or Liam would do something to scare the damn thing away.

"Maybe this wasn't such a good idea." Mackenzie said, quietly. Analise whipped around and glared at her.

"No shit, Sherlock. Now shut up."

"What if we climb the tree and sit there until something walks by, and then you shoot it? No moving, no talking, no noise."

"Now, that is an idea. You two in that tree,"— Analise pointed to a tree about twenty feet from where she was standing—"and I will go up this one."

Mackenzie just gave her a thumbs up instead of agreeing. She wouldn't say another word. Her and Liam walked over to their appointed tree and climbed up. Once they were there, they realized that the tree branch wasn't nearly as long as they thought. If they were to sit there together, she would have to be practically in his lap.

Liam saw the dilemma, too. But would he go along with it, or was he going to still be standoff-ish for reasons she didn't quite understand? His exaggerated sigh followed by him sitting on the thick branch first told her all she needed to know. She tried to hide her smile as she placed herself in his lap.

A soft rumble erupted from his chest and a shiver ran down her spine. The closeness was much desired and so hard to contain. His warm breath ghosted across her neck. He held her to him with one arm around her waist and held himself to the tree with the other. Mackenzie placed her own arm on top of his and pressed into him. A sliver of skin on her stomach was peeking out between her shirt and pants. Instantly, his fingers found it. The rough pads of his finger tips rubbed circles on her smooth skin. She was hungry, but not for food.

Mackenzie attempted to turn her head, to capture his lips with hers again. But he pulled back, relaxed his grip, and removed his warm hand from her skin. He leaned in, and very quietly but strongly, said, "Don't."

Swallowing a lump in her throat, she nodded. She needed to talk to him, but it wasn't the time. For the time being, she would have a tough exterior because everything inside of her felt like it was crumbling.

~*~

After the loud bang of the shot gun going off, killing a small animal that would feed them for the rest of the day, there was little sound coming from their camp. The fire crackled, animals in the woods around them spoke to one another, and feet shuffled as they moved about. But no one spoke.

Mackenzie didn't like the silence. It felt as if it was deliberate, and that did not bode well for them as a group. When the sun began to sink behind the trees, Analise got up and walked away. Liam sat up immediately, watching her retreating figure. When his eyes cut to Mackenzie, she could see the worry they held.

"Maybe she needs to pee. No one wants an audience for that. Peeing in the woods is much harder for girls." Mackenzie thought she saw a small smile trying to break through his hard facade.

"If she isn't back in a few minutes, we go and find her."

Mackenzie nodded, and when Analise came back through, she gave Liam a very smug 'told you so' look. He just nodded his head, and returned his gaze to the fire.

Another hour passed, and Mackenzie wanted to scream. The silence was driving her nuts. She looked to Analise, hoping that she could sit with her and strike up a conversation, any conversation, but found her asleep, mouth agape and drooling.

She couldn't help the giggle that bubbled out of her at the sight. Liam looked up, and the smile that broke out on his face was enough to warm her body straight through to her soul. She tried looking at him with hopeful eyes. She wanted him to talk to her, explain to him what she had done. She just hoped he understood what she hadn't figured out how to say with words.

Liam stood and strode over to her. She watched him carefully and scooted over on her log a little, hoping he would take the invitation. He did.

"Did you mean it?" he asked with a strong voice. His limbs were slightly shaking and his eyes held a fear she had never seen in him, but his voice was strong.

"Yes."

"Then why did it take Geoff leaving for you to tell me. I am not a back-up plan, Mac."

"Never. I didn't tell you because I wanted to tell him first. Then everything kept getting in the way. The attacks on my father's pack, him being a dick and asking my father to mate me to him, us getting attacked. I just hadn't found the time. I felt like if I made the time it would be selfish because so much more stuff was going on. My love life is not important compared to people dying. But Liam, I want you. I chose you. I love you."

"This has nothing to do with Geoff?"

"Nothing. I realized that Geoff was just a good friend that I was attracted to physically. Well, he was a friend, or so I thought. But you? Everything about you attracts me. Your smile, your eyes, your laugh, the way you scrunch your nose when you don't like something, the way you light up a room when you do. I love the way I feel when I am with you, and when I'm not, I feel lost. Empty. Not to mention you are pretty good looking." She added the last line to make him smile. He knew he was good looking, but she figured she would throw it out there after saying that about Geoff.

"What took you so long?"

"I didn't want to hurt him. I wanted to keep him as a friend. He helped me when I needed it most, and he protected me when I couldn't protect myself. I had no idea he was the reason behind it all, or at least part of the reason. I knew there was something between us all along, except you know, when you tried killing me and all. I just couldn't let go of the idea that he and I were somehow supposed to find each other. I still think we were. But I think it's because of you. If they had never found me, I never would have found you. It may sound selfish as hell, but for the first time since this whole paranormal bullshit started, I am glad it did. Now that I know you, I wouldn't change a damn thing. Except, maybe the trusting Geoff part."

"Right, that would be a good thing to change."

"Are we okay?"

"More than." Liam leaned forward and crushed his lips to hers. He didn't wait for permission; he didn't gently touch her lips with his tongue asking to be let in. He took what he wanted and she let his tongue dominate her mouth. With a quick nip to her lip, he pulled back and looked her straight in the eyes.

"I love you so goddamn much it hurts."

His words lit her body on fire. Every inch of her erupted with a need to be touched, caressed, taken. A growl ripped from his chest, and a whimper of need from hers. She knew there was no more holding back.

~*~

Mackenzie's heart beat rapidly in her chest as she watched Liam pull his shirt from his body. With wild eyes Liam turned his attention to her, grabbing her around the waist and pulling her into his lap in one swift move.

His lips captured hers once again and Mackenzie groaned into his mouth. She could feel his hard dick beneath her, and she needed more. Without breaking their kiss, she turned her body to face him, straddle him. When he was pressed up against her aching pussy, she growled.

Liam made quick work of her shirt, pulling it up over her head and tossing it to the side, exposing her lace covered breasts. He pulled back, panting from their kiss, to take in the beauty that was her body, before removing that too, and diving into her pliant flesh.

His mouth and tongue traced, kissed, and licked every inch of her breast before taking her pebbled nipple into his mouth. There was nothing gentle about how he sucked her, how he nibbled at her tip, how he thrust his hips up into her core as she sat above him. She didn't want gentle. She ground down on him before latching her teeth to his neck.

Liam released her nipple and stood, picking her up with him, and walked them away from the fire. She wouldn't ask where he was taking her. She didn't care as long as his arms were around her and his cock was pressed into her. If they didn't ditch the rest of the clothing soon, she might explode.

Liam set her on her feet quickly, before working at the button on her jeans. She reached forward and tried to undo his, but a sharp smack of her hand, and a shake of his head, stopped her in her tracks. He undressed her slowly, pulling her pants and underwear down her legs, and allowing his fingers to graze her bare legs. Liam knelt before her naked body and looked up at her with a mischievous glint in his eye.

His arms snaked between her legs and around, gripping her hips with his hands. Mackenzie's own hands found purchase in his hair, her breathing labored, waiting to see what he would do. Liam stood quickly, and lifted her body up, so her most private area was lined up with his mouth.

Her pussy was wet in anticipation of what was to come just as her back hit the rough bark of a tree. Liam leaned forward, letting the tip of his tongue trace her slit up and down, once, twice, a third time. Mackenzie couldn't take the teasing any longer and used her grip on his head to push him into her. His mouth enveloped her heat.

Liam sucked her clit into his mouth and flicked it with his tongue. The contrast of his ministrations on her body with the scratching from the tree on her back tipped her over the orgasmic edge. Mackenzie cried out, her body shaking from pleasure.

Liam didn't stop. Her clit was throbbing, and just when she thought she couldn't take anymore, he bit down on her. Blinding pleasure coursed through her body, tensing all of her muscles at once. When she could see again, her eyes were fixed on Liam. Mackenzie licked her lips and pushed at him, forcing him away from her as she righted herself on the ground.

Liam quickly removed his own clothing and stood before her hard as a rock. His naked body, even hard, wasn't new to her, but the hunger she felt for him always, felt stronger than the time before.

Mackenzie stalked forward and gripped his dick in one hand, and his neck in the other. She pulled his head to her, and kissed him as she pumped his cock with the other. She could feel the pulsing under her hand begin to speed with every stroke. He was close, but she wanted to feel his cock inside of her.

She released him, and the two dropped to the ground. Liam knelt over her body, and stared into her eyes. All the hard and fast passion that had been there before vanished, and what remained was pure love and adoration. Slowly he leaned in and kissed her. Soft and sensual. Mackenzie lifted one leg and hooked it around his hip while tracing the contours of his back with her hands. When his hardened length touched her opening, she smiled into his mouth.

He slowly entered her, sheathing himself completely. He pulled back and thrust forward again, filling her. Mackenzie's head flew backwards and her eyes closed. Liam continued on, growing faster and harder with each stroke. His lips traveled from her lips to her neck and back again.

Liam's thrusts became erratic and frenzied. She could feel her own muscles tensing in extreme pleasure; she could feel the pressure building up inside of her, desperately begging to be released. Mackenzie opened her eyes to look into his. She wanted to watch him fall over the edge with her, inside of her.

"I love you," he whispered before a groan escaped him. Those words, and how he made her feel in that moment, allowed the damn to burst, sending her body into wondrous convulsions beneath him.

"I love you, too," she said right back. Liam's body slumped atop of hers, covered in sweat and sex.

TWENTY-SIX

Mackenzie awoke wrapped in Liam's arms. She smiled and snuggled in tighter to his chest. She could feel the rhythmic rise and fall of his chest match up perfectly with little snores.

"You look perfectly comfy over there and all, but I could use a hand with breakfast, if we plan on heading out any time soon," Analise said. Mackenzie sat up right in a hurry, and as her eyes adjusted to the morning light, she scanned the area. She and Liam never made it back to the fire before falling asleep. They didn't even manage to get dressed.

Flushing a crimson red, Mackenzie began searching for her clothing. Nudity wasn't unusual around Werewolves, but it typically was because of a moon cycle, and not getting caught the morning after amazing sex.

"Sorry, uh, yeah. Have you seen my bra?" Asking the question was almost as humiliating as Analise knowing exactly what they were up to the night before.

"You mean this?" She held Mackenzie's bra up by the strap dangling off her finger. Then she shot it at her like a sling shot. "I am glad you two worked out whatever the hell that was yesterday. I was going nuts in all that silence. But next time? Can we keep the moaning and growls to a lower decibel?"

"You heard us?" Mackenzie asked in horror.

"Honey, I think the whole damn state could hear you."

"Oh, God."

Analise laughed and poked the fire. "Hurry up, let's eat and get moving. I'm looking forward to meeting your pop."

Mackenzie just nodded and dressed. She also collected Liam's clothing and set it beside him for when he woke.

Heating up the leftover meat from the night before was quick. Mackenzie walked over to Liam and knelt beside him. He looked so peaceful while he slept. His blonde hair and long eyelashes made him look so innocent. She leaned in close and whispered his name and words of love, before softly kissing his lips, his nose, and his forehead. She was pretty sure he was awake by the change in his breathing, but continued on anyway.

Only once she had covered his face in kisses, did he open his eyes.

"I think I need to be woken like that every morning."

"I think that can be arranged."

~*~

Retracing their steps back to her father's camp was harder than any of them expected. Mackenzie had been knocked out cold for part of the trip after the battle with Margret's-Geoff's-men. Liam apparently had been so focused on her that he hadn't paid much attention, and Analise didn't know where she was going at all.

After two days, Mackenzie was ready to say 'fuck it' and give up on the plan of finding her father. A deep sinking feeling filled her. If she couldn't find him after just a few days, how would she ever find him in the future? How would she find her sister?

"Don't worry, we have to be close. Take a deep breath in. Smell that?" Liam asked while rubbing comforting circles on her back.

"Is that exhaust?"

"Thank god! Civilization!" Analise shouted and ran toward the offending smell. The closer they got, the louder the cars.

When they emerged from the trees, they stood on the side of a busy highway. Looking in both directions, Mackenzie wasn't quite sure where they were.

"Which way?" she asked.

"Um. Left. Let's go left," Analise said and started walking in that direction. Mackenzie wished her wolf came with a sense of direction. She couldn't tell which way they were headed. Was the highway a west/east or a north/south?

"Wait. I know where we are!" Liam shouted. He pointed across the highway to a tourist sign for some dinner at the next exit.

"You've been here before?"

"The diner! That's the same place your dad brought us food from the first night we were there. We head into town and start sniffing around. We'll find them in no time."

" Look at you, body of a wolf, brain of an elephant!" Analise said as she jogged back over to them. When the coast was clear, they ran across the highway, and happily walked the three miles to the next exit.

Once they were in town, they didn't need to find Mackenzie's father. His pack found them.

~*~

Darren's men had been out 'patrolling' the town, keeping an eye out for any unusual or unknown Were to come through. They were taking as many precautions as possible, and when Mackenzie, Liam, and Analise came strolling through less than a week after they left, they knew there was a problem.

The three were rushed to a large brown house that sat on a corner lot. As they approached, Mackenzie could hear children laughing and running about the house. Smiling in spite of the situation, she hoped to see her sister. Maybe while they were there, they could finish playing Barbies.

Liam enveloped her hand in his and led the way up the front steps. Kevin, the Were who found them, pushed the door open. He didn't have a chance to even announce their presence before her father came bolting down the stairs in the entryway.

"What's wrong? What happened?" Darren asked in a rush before his feet even hit the bottom step.

"We were right." Liam was matter of fact. There was no emotion to his words. It was as if he had shut them off. Mackenzie didn't understand how he could do it. She wished she did. No matter how great it was, and how full her heart was with him, she still held onto the hurt and anger that Geoff left behind.

Darren's eyes blazed and a scream that sounded almost like a growl bellowed from him. He turned and gripped the banister and pulled. The wood fell away, leaving splinters and sawdust in its wake. Darren threw the banister into the wall, and walked directly in front of Mackenzie, his chest heaving.

For the first time, she was frightened of her father. She had brought this on them. She had endangered his pack. What could, possibly, one day be her pack. She waited for the sting of his hand, but it never came. Instead, she was tugged into his chest and wrapped in Darren's strong embrace. "Thank God you're okay. I'm going to kill him."

Mackenzie hugged her father back, relieved he wasn't angry with her, even if she did deserve it. The looks the other members in the house were giving her were not as forgiving as her father's.

Darren pulled back, and shook Liam's hand, then looked to Analise. With a welcoming smile he asked, "And who might this be?"

"Dad, this is Analise. She was the other bitten I told you about. The one that went to California, then left the pack."

"Right, Analise. Welcome. I would love to be able to sit and get to know you better, but I think we have more pressing matters to attend to."

"Yes, sir. I agree," Analise said with a smile. She wasn't offended. She wanted this whole Margret thing over just as much as the rest of them.

The pack mulled around the doorway to the sitting room that Darren led them to. When the story unfolded again, Mackenzie couldn't control the tears. So many lives lost, so much betrayal, and she was at the center of it. No matter what it took, she would fix it. Even if that meant figuring out how to kill Margret herself.

"So what do we do?"

"We build an army. We gather as many packs as we can who will stand up against her, against her evil monarchy, and we fight. We don't wait for her to come to us. We go after her." Darren was in full pack leader protector mode. He was pacing the room, wringing his hands, with eyes of steal staring at a placard on the wall. Mackenzie hadn't actually taken the time to look around when they first came in, but it was a large and intricate graphic.

Standing, she moved next to her father, placing a hand on his arm to stop his pacing, and stared at the wall where he was.

It wasn't just any graphic. It was a chart. A bloodline chart.

"We go to the most well known and well respected packs first. If we get them on board, if we get them to believe what you are saying and that you are not actually with her, the rest will follow."

"But how do we find them?" Mackenzie asked.

"You start at the top."

~*~

They had to move quick. If Margret and Geoff were going to speed up their efforts, there wasn't a second to waste. Once a plan had been decided on, it was a flurry of activity. Plane tickets were bought, bags were packed, and passports were forged.

Mackenzie was going to get to see the world like she always wanted. Too bad it was going to be spent on a mission to find her royal relatives instead of sightseeing. At least Liam would be with her.

Analise was going to stay with the pack. As far as anyone could tell, she didn't have the extra abilities that pointed to royal blood. Plus, she had insider information that could be helpful to Darren and his fighters who were going to be training night and day in preparation.

Liam and Mackenzie said their goodbyes, and with a single bag each, climbed into a cab headed for the nearest international airport.

"Are you ready for this?" Mackenzie asked.

"Ready for what? To finish what we started?"

"Not just that. What if we find a direct descendant of yours? Will that freak you out?"

"At this point, I don't think much would freak me out. I think with everything we have been through, knowing that I actually have something inside of me that will help, will be a welcome relief."

"You don't need royal blood. You already have something inside of you. Courage. Heart. Love. Strength. Pick one. They're all there."

Liam leaned in and kissed her softly. When they pulled apart, the cab was pulling up to the curb of the airport. Liam handed cash over to pay their fare.

"Thanks. So where you two lovebirds off to?" the cabby asked.

"France," they said in unison.

ABOUT THE AUTHOR

 Growing up, Adrianne couldn't get her hands on enough books to satisfy her need for the make believe. If she finished a novel and didn't have a new one ready and waiting for her, she began to create her own tales of magic and wonder. Now, as an adult, books still make up majority of her free time, and now her tales get written down to be shared with the world.

During the day, Adrianne uses her camera to capture life's stories for clients of all ages and at night, after her two children are tucked in bed; she devotes herself to her written work. Adrianne is living the life she always wanted, surrounded by art and beauty, the written word and a loving family.

As a young adult and new adult author, Adrianne James has plans to bring stories of growing characters, a little romance, and perhaps a little magic and mythology down the line for her readers to enjoy.

FIND ADRIANNE ON THE WEB
www.AdrianneJames.com

www.Facebook.com/AuthorAdrianneJames

www.Twitter.com/Adrianne_James